School Stories
for Seven Year Olds

Helen Paiba is known as one of the most committed, knowledgeable and acclaimed children's booksellers in Britain. For more than twenty years she owned and ran the Children's Bookshop in Muswell Hill, London, which under her guidance gained a superb reputation for its range of children's books and for the advice available to its customers.

Helen was involved with the Booksellers Association for many years and served on both its Children's Bookselling Group and the Trade Practices Committee. In 1995 she was given honorary life membership of the Booksellers Association of Great Britain and Ireland in recognition of her outstanding services to the association and to the book trade. In the same year the Children's Book Circle (sponsored by Books for Children) honoured her with the Eleanor Farjeon Award, given for distinguished service to the world of children's books.

She retired in 1995 and now lives in London.

School

STORIES

for Seven Year Olds

COMPILED BY HELEN PAIBA

ILLUSTRATED BY BEN CORT

MACMILLAN
CHILDREN'S BOOKS

First published 2001 by Macmillan Children's Books
a division of Pan Macmillan Limited
20 New Wharf Road, London N1 9RR
Basingstoke and Oxford
www.panmacmillan.com

Associated companies throughout the world

ISBN 0 330 48378 1

1 3 5 7 9 8 6 4 2

A CIP catalogue record for this book is available
from the British Library.

Typeset by SX Composing DTP, Rayleigh, Essex
Printed and bound in Great Britain by
Mackays of Chatham plc, Kent

Contents

Miss Parson's Pet

W. J. Corbett

Little Joe Bloggs lived under a hill overlooking the school. Every morning he gazed out of his turf spy hole and watched the children trooping through the gates to tackle their lessons. Little Joe was in love with the idea of going to school. He yearned to wear a school scarf and carry a satchel bulging with books. He was certain he would be clever at lessons and brilliant at sport if only he could be a real pupil. He blurted out his hopes and dreams to his parents.

"You wouldn't fit in," warned his father. "Our sort have never been welcome in human society."

"Nonsense," said Mother. "Our little Joe is as good as any child. I say we enrol him for the

1

next term. We'll soon get him a proper coloured scarf and a satchel. And we've got plenty of dusty books on our shelves to make him look business-like. Why should our son have to hide himself away just because he looks a bit different?"

"Very well," sighed Father. "But I can see trouble ahead."

Little Joe beamed his beautiful smile. At last his dream was about to come true. In his mind he was already top of the class in everything.

"Remember, Little Joe," said his mother, "when joining a school one must always show respect by taking the teacher a small gift. And one must always wear a smile even though things are going badly. You can always weep your heart out when you get home, if you have to."

"Also, very important," said his worried father, "never be late for your first day at school."

But because of the enormous weight of his satchel, Little Joe was . . .

*

The children were back after the long summer break. There was lots of jostling and excited talk in the corridor as friends swapped holiday snaps and compared suntans. There was also much nudging and glancing at the shy newcomers who were pretending not to be new at all. Suddenly there was a hush as Miss Parsons came striding down the corridor, her arms piled high with papers and books. The old dragon had arrived to spoil everyone's day.

"No gathering in herds," she snapped, unlocking the classroom door. "File inside and sit down quietly."

There were twenty desks in the classroom. After some quarrelling and chair-leg scraping, nineteen were filled. In the meantime Miss Parsons had arranged herself at her high desk.

"The register," she said, opening her ledger and unscrewing the top from her fountain-pen. "Starting at the front, call out your names and addresses in a clear voice. And there will be no giggling. There is nothing amusing about a name and address. First . . ."

"John Wayne Brown," said the boy, blushing. "Number seven, Poplar Road. But they call me Jack, Miss Parsons."

The class stifled their giggles as Miss Parsons entered the details in her book. "And the next?"

"Madonna Monroe," said Maddy, biting her lip. "Number twenty-one, Elmtree Avenue. But—"

"I'm not here to enter 'buts' in my register," said Miss Parsons, glaring. She carried on round the class until everyone was entered and blotted. She was just about to slam her book shut when she noticed something. Taking off her glasses she polished them and peered again. She began to look very annoyed. It was just as well the cane had been banned from the school.

"We have a joker," she snapped. "There are twenty desks in my classroom and only nineteen names in my register."

"That's because one of the desks is empty, Miss Parsons," said Jack, turning to point.

"The desk at the back by the door. The desk nobody wants."

Just then the door squeaked open and in shuffled the missing pupil. Around his neck he wore a brand-new school scarf, and he was lugging the heaviest satchel any child had ever seen. He bore no trace of suntan. This was because he was bright orange from the top of his crested head to the tip of his long curling tail. His toenails were enormously long which was probably why he wasn't wearing ordinary trainers like everyone else.

Watched by the astonished children he waddled down the aisle between the desks to Miss Parson's high perch. Dipping an orange claw into his satchel he produced a rosy-red apple which he placed on the teacher's blotting pad. Then beaming all over his orange face he lumbered back to squeeze his fat body into the seat behind the empty desk, wrapping his long tail around his midriff.

"Are we dreaming?" asked Jack in a whisper.

If Jack was dreaming the orange pupil certainly wasn't. Again his claw delved into his bulging satchel. His cleverness shrieked out to every child in the class as he stacked *The Complete Works of Shakespeare* on his desk. Then he leant back in his seat and gazed adoringly at Miss Parsons, as if eager to be taught something he didn't already know.

"I was just about to close my register," said Miss Parsons. But her eyes were kind behind her spectacles. "Just don't be late again. And now call out your name and address."

"Little Joe Bloggs," said the latecomer in a clear voice. "From under the hill at the back of the school."

"Thank heavens for a good plain name," murmured Miss Parsons as she wrote the facts down and blotted them.

"But, Miss Parsons," shouted Maddy, springing to her feet. "You've just entered a dragon in your register. He isn't a proper child like us. His Shakespeare books speak volumes. No ordinary pupil can quote *Hamlet* and be bright orange at the same time. If Little Joe Bloggs isn't a dragon pretending to be a child then me and the class don't know nothing."

"Certainly not grammar," winced Miss Parsons. "I despair for your future, Madonna Monroe. I hope you do better in English this term for the sake of your job prospects."

Madonna pouted and sat down.

Little Joe was still beaming but looking a bit puzzled. He had been expecting his schooldays to be the happiest days of his life. He had hoped to be firm friends with all his schoolmates by now. So where was all the ragging and joking he was longing to be part of? His lovely smile faltered as another pupil stood up to say more nasty things.

"Miss Parsons," said Jack. "We children are simply saying that Little Joe Bloggs doesn't fit into our school. No genuine child would come to school with an apple for the teacher. He may be a creep and a Shakespeare genius, but he'll always be an orange dragon to us."

"Silence!" ordered Miss Parsons. "I will not have jealousy and name-calling in my classroom. Little Joe is now in my register which means he is entitled to a superior education. A dragon indeed. Little Joe Bloggs is a bright little boy who's come to school to learn like anyone else. And there's a lesson for you all. For it's pupils like him who get dozens of A-levels and go on to row the boat for Oxford. Now, I insist that you all turn around in your seats and apologize to him for your rudeness and bad manners."

As she spoke the truth dawned on the children. While they saw an orange dragon beaming behind a pile of clever books, Miss Parsons saw only a polite and eager pupil who was going to put everyone else at the bottom of the class. They howled with disbelief and envy, but their teacher was unmoved. Pointing her pen at the loudest protesters she warned, "Do as I say unless you want to be sent home with Black Spot letters to show your parents."

The threat of the dreaded Black Spot letter quelled all but the bravest heart. The cowed children turned around in their seats and chorused, "We apologize for calling you a creepy orange dragon, Little Joe . . ."

Little Joe's lumpy face creased into a joyful grin. At last he felt a friend amongst friends. He began planning the first practical joke he would play in the playground. Then . . .

"Even though I'm forced to apologize, he's still an ugly orange dragon," shouted a defiant lad. "You wait till we get you at playtime, Bloggsy."

"Nor will I tolerate bullying, Elvis Johnson," snapped Miss Parsons. Swiftly she scrawled a fountain-pen letter and sealed it in an envelope. Then, watched by every eye, she licked and stuck on a terrible Black Spot. With a crooked finger she beckoned Elvis to her desk. "You are banned from school for the rest of the day. Take this letter home for your parents to read. And when you report back in the morning I want to see one hundred neatly written lines that read, 'I must not call my classmate an ugly orange dragon', and take off that insolent cap when you approach my desk."

Elvis pulled off his beloved baseball cap and slouched to Miss Parson's desk. Stuffing the Black Spot letter into his back pocket he shambled from the room, slamming the door behind him. During the shocked silence that followed, Little Joe made another terrible mistake. He began to clap and cheer and beam even wider. In his mind the class apology and the sending home of Elvis meant he was now one of the gang. He was wrong. The children began to jeer at him. They were determined that a smarmy dragon would never become one of their in-crowd . . .

"Miss Parsons!" cried Maddy. "Please give me a Black Spot letter too, because I refuse to stay in this classroom with a smirking, clapping dragon."

"That's how I feel," yelled Jack.

"We all do," shouted the angry children.

"Apart from me," said a little girl at the front. "My mum and dad will kill me if I miss a day from school. Anyway, I reckon I can beat Little Joe in the exams if I swot hard enough."

But hers was a lone voice drowned by stamping trainers and catcalls.

"Silence!" thundered Miss Parsons. "This is a place of study not a football stadium. Open your history books at page twelve. This morning we are going to discuss the Dark Ages."

"No, we're not," shouted Maddy. "Because, Miss Parsons, if you don't chuck that ugly

Little Joe out on his ear, we are going on strike."

"That's what I was going to say," yelled Jack.

"I'm not going on strike," said the worried little girl at the front. "I've got too much to learn and too much to lose if I step out of line."

But the rest of the children were herding behind Maddy and Jack. They were all on their feet actually challenging the stern authority of Miss Parsons.

"Very well, get out of my classroom," she stormed. "For the sensible ones who wish to stay the Dark Ages lesson will continue as normal."

Seventeen defiant children marched out of the classroom. In no time at all they were gathered in the playground waving hastily chalked banners that read:

WHAT DO WE WANT? DRAGONS OUT.
WHEN DO WE WANT IT? NOW.

Miss Parsons ignored them. Her job was to

teach obedient children, not to pacify an unruly mob. Though deep down she felt sad. Outside were so many bright pupils, capable of so much. What a pity they directed their energies into protesting against Little Joe Bloggs because of his unfortunate appearance and his eagerness to learn. For Miss Parsons refused to allow race, or creed or colour to interfere with her love for teaching. She saw a pupil and she taught. But there was one small chink in her armour. She knew that the children called her 'the old dragon' behind her back. That could have been one reason why she sided with Little Joe. But, ignoring the clamour outside the classroom window, she continued to do what she did best – teach – even though her class now only numbered two.

"Now, back to lessons," she said. "Who can tell me something about the time we call the Dark Ages?"

The little girl shot up her hand and began to reel off dates and the names of legendary kings her ambitious parents had drummed into her head.

"Very good," said Miss Parsons. Then she turned to Little Joe who was bravely smiling through his tears in his back seat by the door. "And you, Little Joe, can you tell us a little about that dark period?"

"There were dragons in those days, Miss Parsons," said Little Joe, wiping his eyes on the back of his orange claw. "And the dragons who lived then were hated just as much as they are today."

"History is mostly sad, Little Joe," said Miss Parsons, gently. "As is the present, but hopefully not the future."

And the learning and the lessons went on in spite of the noisy crowd outside. Just before the lunch bell rang Miss Parsons made a little speech.

"Because you've both been so attentive in spite of the noise outside, I'm going to award you each a Gold Star to put in your exercise books."

What an honour.

The two pupils looked suitably shy as she

awarded them their sticky-backed stars. Then she said that as this was the first day of term it was her duty to select the Class Prefect, and her choice was Little Joe. As she gravely pinned the badge on his scarf Little Joe's delight spilt over. He beamed and punched the air with an orange fist and gave a friendly thumbs-up sign to the little girl. Alas, Little Joe had a lot to learn about the moods and tantrums of other children. They rarely smiled through their tears as he had been taught to do. For suddenly the little girl was on her feet, her eyes flashing with anger at the choice.

"I refuse to accept Little Joe as Prefect, Miss Parsons," she raged. "I need that badge much more than he does. My mum and dad wanted me to become Class Prefect. If I go home a loser they'll make my life a misery."

"As a teacher, *I* choose the Class Prefect," said Miss Parsons, firmly. "Now, sit down at once."

"Won't," said the girl, flouncing from the classroom. "I'm going on strike with the others. I've got nothing to lose any more."

And so they were two, Miss Parsons sitting at her high desk, Little Joe sitting at the back of the room wearing a meek smile. Then the lunch bell rang.

"In spite of all that fuss lessons will resume promptly after lunch," said Miss Parsons, gathering up her books and papers and the apple and sweeping from the classroom. "And don't be late a second time, Little Joe Bloggs."

The banners were stacked against the playground wall. Not even a strike was going to interfere with the serious task of playing. This was their own time, after all. As they yelled and cheered and dashed about they totally ignored Little Joe who squatted all alone eating his banana and sardine sandwiches. He yearned to play in goal between the two sweaters. He would even have enjoyed playing bounce the ball against the wall if only the girls had asked him. But they didn't. Still smiling he offered a sandwich to anyone who came near. But this generosity was snootily refused. He was the only pupil to return to the classroom when lunch time ended. The others had picked up their banners and were striking again . . .

"Dragons out . . . dragons out . . ." they chanted outside the classroom window as Little Joe sat miserably at his desk, watching Miss Parsons chalk some numbers on her blackboard.

"This afternoon will be devoted to arithmetic," she announced. "What can you tell me about the exciting mystery of numbers, Little Joe?"

But the small dragon was only concerned with one sum. That morning there had been twenty pupils. One had been sent home with a Black Spot letter, leaving nineteen.

Then seventeen had walked out on strike leaving two. Finally, another had stormed out, leaving one. Those were the figures the small dragon summed up in his mind. And the answer? That he was easily the most hated classmate in the world. It was no wonder he could barely smile now. Deep down Little Joe had never been mad keen to be a genius and go on to row for Oxford. He had simply been in love with the idea of going to school and having lots of friends to joke with. Now here he was all alone in the classroom with no one to throw paper darts at.

"Are you paying attention, Little Joe?" asked Miss Parsons sharply. "Never mind gazing out of the window at that noisy crowd. Just ignore them and copy down the numbers on my blackboard into your exercise book."

But Little Joe wasn't listening. An extra wide smile was spreading across his orange face as an idea dawned. Clattering back his chair he waddled from the classroom as fast as he could.

"Where are you going?" shouted Miss Parsons. "Come back here unless you want a Black Spot letter."

Outside in the playground Jack and Maddy were sharing a banner and leading the chanting. Then to their astonishment they saw Little Joe approaching, his face determined. Parking himself in front of their banner he raised an orange claw and brandished it at the classroom window.

"WHAT DO WE WANT? DRAGONS OUT. WHEN DO WE WANT IT? NOW," he yelled at the top of his voice. Everyone fell silent, their mouths agape. Finally Jack found the words.

"What are you doing here, Little Joe?" he asked. "This strike is to get you chucked out of school. You can't demonstrate against

yourself. The rules of striking don't allow it."

Everyone nodded in agreement.

"How can we chuck you out while you're trying to chuck yourself out?" argued Maddy.

Little Joe hung his head. His idea had come unstuck. He had hoped to win their hearts by supporting their cause, even if it was against himself. But you can't become one of the gang simply by joining them. You need to be accepted, and this Little Joe didn't understand, having never been to school before.

"Get back to your precious Miss Parsons, Little Joe," shouted his girl rival. "She'll soon strip you of your Class Prefect's badge when she gets hold of you. She's probably already torn the Gold Star from your exercise book. Well, she won't get mine because my book is tucked down the back of my jeans."

"Class Prefect, eh," said Jack, gazing in surprise at the badge on Little Joe's scarf. "And a Gold Star winner too. Well, well."

"And him just an ugly old dragon," scoffed the little girl.

"No, he's not," snapped Maddy. She clapped

her hands to her mouth when she realized what she had said.

"What does that mean?" asked Jack, curiously.

"Well, I think I like him," said Maddy, looking sheepish. "I know he's a dragon but he's beginning to be just Little Joe to me."

"And who can claim to be perfect in looks?" agreed some other children. "Some of us have knobbly knees and toes that turn in, and noses that turn up too much, but we aren't persecuted for being orange with a long tail like Little Joe. We should be striking against ourselves for being so cruel."

"That's true," said Jack. "And I must admit that Little Joe is a good sport. He's the only dragon I know who'd join in a strike against himself."

"You only know one dragon," shouted someone. "And that's Little Joe, who deserves to be one of our gang."

"Very well," said Jack, grinning. "We'll have a vote. Hands up those who want to go back into class with Little Joe."

Eighteen beaming children shot up their hands. Including Little Joe who was voting for himself just like before. For it was being accepted that mattered, and his idea had won out. The little girl raised her hand reluctantly. But because she wasn't beaming like the rest her vote didn't count.

"Right," said Jack, smiling and bowing to Little Joe. "As our Class Prefect you must lead us back into the classroom. That way you'll get the first tongue-lashing from Miss Parsons."

"So," said Miss Parsons, glaring at them as they filed into their seats. "You've all decided to honour me with your presence again."

"It was all a mistake, Miss Parsons," explained Maddy. "We realized outside that we were wrong to turn against Little Joe. Deep down he isn't an ugly dragon at all. He's just the same as us, but a different shape and colour."

"So, the strike is over, Miss Parsons," said Jack. "And we're all very sorry for disrupting your teaching."

"Disrupting your learning, you mean," corrected Miss Parsons. Then she leant from her high desk and pointed her pen from pupil to pupil. "Today I have awarded one Black Spot, two Gold Stars and a Class Prefect's badge. I'm not going to take them back but I'm warning you all. One more squeak from any of you and I'll be writing letters and sticking Black Spots for the rest of this afternoon. Is that understood?"

"Yes, Miss Parsons," chorused the class. Little Joe's 'yes' was the happiest and loudest of all, for at last he had been accepted.

"But just in case you haven't got the message we are going to do arithmetic for the rest of the day," said the teacher. But she was smiling behind her spectacles as she said it.

The class gave a mighty groan but buckled down good-naturedly. And so started and ended the first day of school for Little Joe Bloggs who lived under the hill behind the school.

"You're late home, Little Joe," said his anxious mother. "Your banana and sardine sandwiches are curling up at the edges."

"How did it go, son?" asked his worried father. "You weren't bullied? I warned you that they don't take kindly to the likes of us."

"It's the weight of all the Shakespeare books," winced Little Joe, thumping down his satchel. Then his eyes shone as he rummaged inside. Triumphantly he produced his exercise book with its gleaming Gold Star. Then he showed them his scarf bearing the Class Prefect's badge. And to make things perfect for his father, there wasn't one sign that his son had been bullied.

"Father," said proud Mother. "Not only has our Little Joe been accepted but he's won a Gold Star for excellence. And topping that, he's been made Class Prefect. I always knew we were raising a genius. He'll be rowing the boat for Oxford before we know it. Tomorrow we'll ditch the Shakespeare books and slip a few slim volumes of Plato in his satchel, instead. That should lighten the burden. But, oh Father, isn't it wonderful to know that all our worries were unfounded?"

"Not quite, Mum," said Little Joe. He looked almost proud as he went on. "For I haven't told you about the Black Spot letter I might be sent home with if I'm late again. Miss Parsons said, 'To be late once is annoying, to be late twice is seriously vexing, but to be late three times in a row will not be tolerated, and can only be cured by a Black Spot letter.'"

"So we'll have to get you up earlier," said his mother, making fresh banana and sardine sandwiches.

And they did. Up at the crack of dawn was Little Joe. But he was still late for school that morning. This time it was because of the enormous stack of comics he had stuffed into his satchel to dole out to his brand-new friends.

Perhaps Miss Parsons let him off one more time, perhaps she didn't. But there was no doubt that these schooldays were the happiest of times for a beaming, orange dragon called Little Joe Bloggs.

The Ghost Gorilla

Chris Powling

A ghost gorilla . . .

Can you imagine such a thing? Huge and hairy, with sad gorilla eyes and rippling gorilla muscles, yet – at the same time – horribly, *horribly* invisible?

No, I couldn't believe it, either.

Actually, I was pretty sure it was a joke from the moment Darcy brought it to school. Darcy was that kind of kid. The trouble was, he *agreed* it was a joke straight away. "That's a brilliant goldfish," he said to my best friend Mel as he came up to us in the playground. "And your stick insect is great, Sara! Got a name, has it?"

"Twiggy," I told him.

"And this is Goldie," said Mel.

Already we were goggle-eyed.

What grabbed our attention was the collar – the enormous, silver-studded collar – that Darcy was dangling in the air from the end of an old broomstick. Fixed to the front of the collar was a silver bell. It tinkled eerily as the collar swayed to and fro. "What's that for, Darcy?" Mel asked.

Darcy looked up and bit his lip. "That," he said. "Oh . . . nothing. Just a bit of a joke."

"A joke?" I asked.

"Well . . . a *sort* of joke, Sara," Darcy replied.

By now, of course, other kids had come over. Soon we were all gawping at the collar.

Darcy took no notice of this whatsoever. "Is that your budgie, Elroy?" he exclaimed. "It's terrific! And I really like your gerbil, Nina. Daki's slow-worm is smashing too. It's going to be really tough for Miss Westcott to choose which of them is best."

"Best *looked-after*, Darcy," I reminded him. "That's what the project is all about."

"Best looked after, yes," Darcy agreed. "That's what I meant, Sara."

Tinkle-tinkle-tinkle! went the silver bell.

Still everyone stared. And still Darcy took no notice. He was so busy admiring Josh's terrapins and Razia's white mice he seemed to have forgotten completely that he had a collar, big enough to fit a St Bernard, hanging from his broomstick like a weird, doggy halo.

Tinkle-tinkle-tinkle! the silver bell went.

Of course, by this time, no one wanted to notice it. What worried us was falling for one of Darcy's tricks – and then being teased about it for the rest of term. We'd all seen that happen, thank you. So we pretended to be fascinated by each other's pets, absolutely fascinated, as if the last thing in the world that interested us was Darcy and his floating dog-collar.

Eventually, it was a little kid who came to our rescue. "Darcy," he piped up. "Is that a kite or what?"

"A kite?" said Darcy.

He looked all round for something kite-like till, as if by accident, he caught sight of the dog-collar. "Oh, *that*," he said. "No, that's not a kite. That's my gorilla."

"Gorilla?" the little kid blinked.

"The collar's round his neck," Darcy told him. "Don't worry, though. He isn't real. Actually, he's only a ghost gorilla."

"A ghost gorilla!" gasped the little kid. He took a hasty step backwards.

To tell the truth, he wasn't the only one.

What was so scary was the matter-of-fact way Darcy said it. It was as if the last thing he wanted to do was frighten us. "He won't hurt you," he promised. "All he wants to do is haunt you – you know, give you the creeps an' such. Just like an ordinary ghost, really. Of course, he's a lot *stronger* than an ordinary ghost."

"How do you know?" Razia asked.

"Know what?"

"How do you know he's stronger than an ordinary ghost – when you can't even see him?"

"Because he's a gorilla," said Darcy. "A gorilla is stronger than a person, yes? So a ghost gorilla is bound to be stronger than a ghost person. It stands to reason."

"Yeah . . ." said Razia.

"Hold on," I said. "You told Mel and me that this is just one of your jokes, Darcy."

"It is," said Darcy.

"A joke, right?"

Darcy nodded quickly. "Quite right, Sara. I admit it."

Tinkle-tinkle-tinkle! went the silver bell.

It didn't seem like a joke. Darcy made sure of that by shifting his eyes warily over the space where the ghost gorilla was – would have been, I mean. Honestly, what a con-artist! "Look," I said, stepping forward. "I'm waving my hands under the broomstick, see. There's nothing there."

"True," said Darcy.

"But you can walk *through* a ghost, Sara," Mel pointed out.

"Or a ghost can walk through you," Darcy added.

And, just above our heads, he traced a slow circle in the air with the silver-studded collar.

It was amazing.

For a split second, I swear I heard the snort of hot gorilla breath on my cheek and the shuffle of massive gorilla feet almost stepping on mine. "Only a joke," said Darcy.

The little kid started to cry.

Luckily, that's when the bell rang. The school bell, that is, not Darcy's. As we scrambled into the classroom, though, I couldn't help seeing how Darcy hung back a bit, both hands round his broomstick, while kids who should have known better cleared a space all round him for the ghost gorilla. "Just look at him," I snarled. "He's fooling the lot of them!"

"Yeah . . ." said Mel.

I glared at her in disgust. Was she fooled by Darcy too? "Miss Westcott will soon sort him out," I predicted.

And so she did. "A ghost gorilla?" she sniffed, when Darcy had explained. "Are you ready to produce a handbook on how to look after him, Darcy? That's part of the project too, you know."

"Certainly, Miss," said Darcy.

"Fine," said Miss Westcott. "I can't wait to see it, Darcy. Now, put your ghost gorilla in the stock cupboard, please. Under lock and key, I think. We don't want him to escape, do we?"

"Er . . . Miss," Darcy said. "He can walk *through* walls, you know. All ghosts can."

"Not these walls, Darcy. These walls

happen to be ghost-proof."

"Ghost gorilla-proof as well, Miss?"

"Exactly, Darcy."

Darcy sighed with relief. "What a stroke of luck!" he said.

After this we settled down to our handbooks – at our desks, on the floor, behind the reading trolley, wherever we could find a space with our pets. Darcy worked by himself in the painting corner. This was strange, really, since it was about as far as he could get from the stock cupboard. Maybe he wanted to forget the ghost gorilla.

Maybe we all did.

But it wasn't easy. Somehow, in the back of our minds, he was always there under lock and key – his knuckles brushing the games equipment on the floor, his head nudging the topmost shelf where we kept the science stuff.

Just before lunch, Miss Westcott came round for a final check on our progress. As usual, she left everyone beaming – everyone, that is, except Darcy. We all fell quiet when we picked up the sharpness in her voice. "As a painting it's excellent, Darcy. I've never seen such a cloudy, steamy rainforest. I asked for a handbook, though – something that tells us how we should care for the creature we've chosen. There's no creature here at all."

"It's too late, Miss," said Darcy sadly. "There's none of them left to see. *All* these gorillas are ghosts."

"Ghosts?"

"Like the one I brought in this morning, Miss." Casually, Darcy glanced across the room.

So did the rest of us.

Except we weren't nearly so casual. Mostly, our eyes were out on stalks. For above the sound of budgies and gerbils and white mice – not to mention a deafening roar here and there from the odd stick insect – we heard through the door of the stock cupboard, faintly but clearly, the ringing of a silver bell.

Tinkle-tinkle-tinkle!

It was Darcy's greatest trick. We all agreed about that even if we couldn't decide how he'd

34

done it. My own theory is that he had help from Miss Westcott herself, who moved the project along to *Endangered Species* a little *too* smoothly in my opinion.

Josie Smith's New Teacher

Magdalen Nabb

O n Sunday night Josie Smith was in the bath with soapsuds all over her hair.

"Ow!" she said, when her mum rubbed too hard. "Ow!"

"Keep still," said Josie's mum. "I have to rub hard because you get so dirty. You could grow potatoes in your ears."

"And cabbages?" asked Josie Smith.

"And cabbages," said Josie's mum. "Now lie back while I rinse you."

"Swim me up and down and sing," said Josie Smith.

So Josie's mum swam her up and down the

bath and rinsed her hair with jugs of water and sang. Josie Smith sang too. Then she got dry. When she was in bed in clean, striped pyjamas, Josie Smith said, "Tomorrow, can I have a ribbon in my hair for school?"

"You'll only lose it," said Josie's mum.

"But can I?" said Josie Smith.

"All right," said Josie's mum. "Now go to sleep."

"And tomorrow," said Josie Smith, "can I take a present for the new teacher? Eileen's taking one."

"And everything Eileen does, you have to do," said Josie's mum.

"But *can* I?" said Josie Smith. "I like my new teacher."

"You can take her an apple," said Josie's mum. "But how do you know you like her if she's only coming tomorrow?"

"She came on Friday," said Josie Smith, "when Miss Ormerod was reading us a story, and she wears nail varnish and perfume."

"Does she now?" said Josie's mum, and she smiled. "Now go to sleep. Ginger's asleep already. Look."

"I can't see him," said Josie Smith. "Move his basket nearer the bed."

Josie's mum moved Ginger's basket and Ginger opened one eye and said, "Eeeiow," and then went to sleep again.

"Why does Ginger say *Eeeiow* instead of Meeiow?" asked Josie Smith.

"I don't know," said Josie's mum. "Now go to sleep."

"Mum?" said Josie Smith.

"What now?" said Josie's mum.

"Will the new teacher know I'm the best at reading and writing?"

"She might," said Josie's mum. "I expect Miss Ormerod will have told her."

"I'm going to write a story for her," said Josie Smith, "in my best writing with no rubbing out because I haven't got a rubber."

"You won't be in a fit state to write anything tomorrow," said Josie's mum, "if you don't get to sleep. It's late."

"I am getting to sleep. Mum?"

"That's enough now," said Josie's mum.

"I'm going down."

"But *Mum*! Can I have a pencil with a rubber at the end like Eileen's?"

"We'll see."

"But can I?"

"I said we'll see. Now go to sleep. I've got some sewing to finish. Goodnight."

And she switched off the light.

"Goodnight!" shouted Josie Smith. Then she whispered to Ginger, "I'm going to think of a story now so I can start it as soon as I get to school."

Josie Smith lay in the dark and thought. She thought of a story with a giant in it. The giant lived in a tower on the top of a hill and when he tried to frighten people he only made them laugh. He was so funny that he made Josie Smith laugh by herself in the dark. She told Ginger about him but Ginger didn't wake up. And downstairs her mum's sewing machine went Tr-r-r-r-r-r-r-ik, tr-r-r-r-r-r-r-ik, tr-r-r-r-r-r-r-ik.

She thought of a better story about a girl who ran away and went to live with the gypsies. The girl had to sleep in a tent and it was dark and cold and rainy and the girl cried because she wanted her mum. Outside in the night, the rain began pattering at Josie Smith's window and tears came to her eyes when she thought about the girl in the gypsy's tent. She told Ginger about it, but Ginger didn't wake up, and downstairs her mum's sewing machine went Tr-r-r-r-r-r-r-ik, tr-r-r-r-r-r-r-ik, tr-r-r-r-r-r-r-ik.

She thought of an even better story with a witch in it. The witch came in at people's windows on rainy nights and stole them when they were asleep. The witch was so frightening that Josie Smith got scared and had to make Ginger wake up to keep her company.

Downstairs, her mum's sewing machine went Tr-r-r-r-r-r-r-ik, tr-r-r-r-r-r-r-ik, tr-r-r-r-r-r-r-ik. Then it stopped. The light came on on the landing and Josie's mum came up to bed.

"Shh!" said Josie Smith to Ginger, and she shut her eyes to pretend she was asleep and then she really was asleep.

"Wake up!" said Josie's mum. "Josie! Didn't you hear me shouting?"

"Is it morning?" said Josie Smith.

"Of course it's morning," said Josie's mum. "You're going to be late for school if you don't hurry up."

Then Josie Smith remembered the new teacher and got dressed as fast as she could. She was so tired that she didn't want her breakfast and when Eileen from next door came to call for her she hadn't got her coat on.

"Hurry up!" said Josie's mum.

Josie Smith got her coat and ran to the front door. Then she came running back.

"My ribbon!" she said. "You promised I could have a hair ribbon!"

"Oh, for goodness' sake," said Josie's mum, and she started looking in the drawers. "Here, this will do."

"I wanted a pink one," said Josie Smith. "Like Eileen's."

"You lost the pink one," said Josie's mum, "like you lose them all. This one's better than a pink one because it matches your kilt."

She tied the ribbon tight in Josie Smith's hair and Josie Smith ran to the front door. Then she came running back.

"My apple!" shouted Josie Smith. "You promised I could take an apple for the new teacher!"

"Oh, for goodness' sake," said Josie's mum. "Here. And don't run or you'll drop it on the way."

Josie Smith ran to the front door and opened it. Eileen was waiting for her. She had two pink ribbons in her hair.

Josie Smith and Eileen set off up the street to school.

"I've got a present for the new teacher," Eileen said.

"So have I," said Josie Smith.

"I'll show you if you want," said Eileen, "only you haven't to touch."

They stopped at a corner and Eileen got the present out of her coat pocket. There was a little coloured box with tissue paper in it and when Eileen opened the tissue paper very carefully Josie Smith saw a brand-new pure white handkerchief with frilly white lace round it and a bunch of pink flowers embroidered in the corner.

"My mum bought it," whispered Eileen, "when she went shopping on Saturday." She folded the tissue paper back and shut the coloured box. Then she said, "What have you got?"

"An apple," said Josie Smith.

"That's not a real present," Eileen said.

"It is," said Josie Smith. "My mum said."

"It's not," said Eileen. "Real presents come from a shop."

"*Well*," said Josie Smith, "apples come from a shop, anyway."

"You got it from your house," said Eileen.

"I'm not going to school with you for being so horrible!" shouted Josie Smith, and she ran off down a back street and hid, holding her apple tight, until Eileen had gone. Then she set off for school by herself.

On the corner next to Josie Smith's school was Mr Scowcroft's allotment where Josie

Smith sometimes went to dig for worms with Gary Grimes. Perhaps Mr Scowcroft would have something good for a present. Mr Scowcroft had some flowers growing at the back of his allotment. They were called pom-pom dahlias. Josie Smith knew what they were called because Mr Scowcroft had told her. Mr Scowcroft was always there in the mornings feeding his hens.

"Mr Scowcroft!" shouted Josie Smith, holding on to the wire fence. "Mr Scowcroft! Can I come in?"

But nobody answered. Mr Scowcroft wasn't there.

Josie Smith thought she'd go in and wait for him. The whistle hadn't gone yet and all the children were playing and shouting in the yard. Mr Scowcroft's gate was locked but there was a hole in the fence. Sometimes his hens got through the hole but they always came back because there was nothing to peck and scratch at in the hard street.

Josie Smith put her apple down and crawled through the hole very carefully so

she wouldn't rip her coat. Then she waited for
Mr Scowcroft near the pom-pom dahlias.
Most of the pom-pom dahlias were dark red
but there were some orange ones and white
ones and a beautiful purple one that Josie
Smith liked very much. She could ask Mr
Scowcroft for the purple one and then dig the
patch for his lettuces after school. Or else she
could dig a bit of it now. All the children were
still playing and shouting in the yard but
Josie Smith didn't want to play with them.
She could dig in the lettuce patch instead

while she was waiting.

Josie Smith got the spade that was leaning on the hen shed and started digging. It was hard work because the spade was big and heavy but the ground was wet and soft and if she stood on the edge of the spade with both her wellingtons it went in.

The children played and shouted in the yard and Josie Smith dug and dug in the allotment until she had dug half the lettuce patch for Mr Scowcroft. Then she stopped. It was so hot that she had to take her coat off, and it was so quiet that she could hear herself getting out of breath. "Phew," she went, "phew-phew-phew." When she got her breath back she said, "That'll be a nice surprise for Mr Scowcroft."

But Mr Scowcroft still didn't come.

"I might as well finish all of it," said Josie Smith to herself, "while I'm waiting." So she dug and dug until all the lettuce patch was done. "Phew," she went, "phew-phew-phew!" Because it was so quiet she could hear herself getting out of breath. When she got her breath back she said, "Now it'll really be a surprise for Mr Scowcroft. I'd better collect the worms for the hens."

Josie Smith didn't like worms. When she came to the allotment with Gary Grimes, she did the digging and he collected the worms. She hated doing it by herself but she got the tin from the hen shed and the handkerchief from her pocket and she used the handkerchief to pick up the worms so that she wouldn't feel them wriggling so much. But when she took the tin of worms to the hen shed she saw that the hen shed was shut. Josie Smith could hear the hens crowing and scuffling and pecking at the door.

"You want your worms, don't you?" said Josie Smith, putting her face near a crack to talk to them.

The hens crowed and scuffled and pecked at the door.

"I expect you heard me digging and now you're hungry."

The hens crowed and scuffled and pecked even harder at the door. But there was a big piece of wood wedged across the door to keep it shut and it looked very heavy to Josie Smith.

"I'd better wait," Josie Smith told the hens through the crack. "I shouldn't open your shed, anyway, because you're Mr Scowcroft's hens." The hens went on crowing and scuffling and pecking just the same. Perhaps they were too daft to know whose hens they were. Once, when Josie Smith asked Mr Scowcroft why the hens pecked at each other, fighting over a worm, and then ran away and forgot to eat it, Mr Scowcroft said, "Because they're daft."

Josie Smith put the worm tin down and went back to look at the purple pom-pom dahlia. She saw a big flower just behind it that wasn't a pom-pom dahlia at all. Josie Smith stood on tiptoe and reached over to pull the big flower's face towards her.

"Ow!" she said. It had prickles. It was a big fat pink rose. When she pulled it towards her it showered raindrops on her face. Josie Smith sniffed. "Perfume!" she whispered.

The rose was soft and cool. But it wasn't Mr Scowcroft's rose. It had poked its head through the wire fence from behind the allotment and come to live with the pom-pom dahlias. Josie Smith had never been behind Mr Scowcroft's allotment. She decided that while she was waiting for Mr Scowcroft she could go and look where the rose came from.

She crawled out through the hole near the gate where she'd left her apple and went round the corner. There was some spare ground next to the allotment where they played cowboys and Indians on the way home from school and a dirt track between the spare ground and Mr Scowcroft's fence. Josie Smith went along the dirt track to the end. She saw some steps going down in the long grass and a fence going down beside it and a gate at the bottom. Josie Smith stopped and listened but there was nobody coming. It was very quiet. She went down the steps. The gate was locked but there was a gap in the fence near the bottom so Josie Smith squeezed through it and stood looking up at the slope behind Mr Scowcroft's allotment.

There were big white rocks all over the slope and all around the rocks there were blue and white and pink flowers growing. Up at the top were the biggest rose bushes that Josie Smith had ever seen. There were more flowers there even than in Mrs Crawshaw's flower shop. Josie Smith started to climb up very carefully. Her wellingtons were wet and slippery with mud and she didn't want to slip off the white rocks and squash the blue and white and pink flowers because they were nice. They were better than buttercups but not as good as bluebells because they didn't smell of anything. Josie Smith went on climbing until she reached the top of the slope right behind the back of the allotment. There were hundreds of pale pink roses full of perfume and raindrops.

"Zzzzzzzzz," said Josie Smith, and put her face into a big pink rose and drank some drops of the bees' drinking water. "Zzzzzzzzz."

Josie Smith chose the biggest rose she

could see and picked it carefully without pricking her fingers too much. When the twig snapped a shower of water and petals fell on her.

"Zzzzzzzzz," said Josie Smith the bee, picking and sniffing and sipping. The soil was very wet under the bushes and her wellingtons sank right in and the petals showered down and covered them. "Pink wellies," said Josie Smith, looking down. Then she said, "Zzzzzzzzz," and picked some more big pink roses. The thorns scratched her hands and the petals stuck to the scratches like plasters and then she felt something go plop on her head. It was too heavy to be a petal or a drop of the bees' drinking water. Josie Smith looked up. The sky was all dirty and dark. Plop! A big squashy raindrop plopped right on Josie Smith's nose. Plop! went another one. Plop plop plop.

"I'd better go now," whispered Josie Smith, "or else I'll get wet. I'll just pick a few more big ones." So she picked a few more big ones and the squashy raindrops went on falling, plopping on the roses and making them nod their heads, bouncing off the leaves and sploshing on to Josie Smith's hands as she chose the best flowers with their petals open wide.

When she couldn't hold any more roses she began to climb down over the rocks in her slippery wellingtons. Once she slipped and hurt her hands but she didn't tread on any of the blue and white and pink flowers.

When she got back to the allotment, Mr Scowcroft still hadn't come. He must have forgotten to come and give the hens their breakfast, Josie Smith thought.

The hungry hens were crowing and scuffling and pecking at the door. I'll have to give them something to eat, thought Josie Smith, or else they'll die. She climbed on an upside-down bucket and pulled and pulled at the big piece of wood across the door until it came loose and fell down. Then she took the tin of worms in to the hens. They crowed and scuffled and pecked at the worms but there weren't enough for everybody and some of the hens didn't get one.

"I could make your breakfast," Josie Smith said, "because I've seen Mr Scowcroft doing it."

But then, all of a sudden, she noticed how quiet it was. She couldn't hear the children shouting and playing in the yard any more. It had been quiet for a long time.

"I have to go to school," she told the hens. "I think it might be late now."

But the hens all stood round Josie Smith, turning their heads to stare at her with one eye, making soft noises and pecking at her wellingtons, wanting their breakfast.

Josie Smith's chest was going bam, bam, bam. She was frightened of being late for school but when she thought of the hens being shut up by themselves in the dark with no breakfast a big lump came in her throat to make her cry. She didn't want the hens to die. She went out and got the bucket and started getting the hens' breakfast from the big bin and mixing it with some water from the barrel. All the time her chest was going bam, bam, bam. Just when she'd finished and shut the door and leant the piece of wood against it, a voice shouted:

"Josie Smith!"

It wasn't Mr Scowcroft. It was Mrs Scowcroft in a long raincoat and wellington boots and carrying an umbrella.

"Whatever are you doing here at this time?" she said. "It's twenty-past nine!"

Twenty-past nine! Josie Smith got hold of her roses and ran past Mrs Scowcroft, through the gate, across the spare ground and into the school yard. She crashed in through the front door and went running and skidding in her slippery muddy wellingtons along the corridor, through the hall and into her classroom. Then she stopped, breathing hard, phew-phew-phew!

Everybody stared. Eileen stared, Gary Grimes stared and Rawley Baxter stared. All the children at the other tables stared. The new teacher stared. And before anybody could say anything, the door burst open behind Josie Smith and a big voice shouted:

"Where's that child?"

Josie Smith turned round. It was Miss Potts, the headmistress, and behind her was Mr Bannister, the caretaker. Miss Potts's face was all red and her eyes were glittery and angry.

"Josie Smith!" she shouted, and Josie Smith's chest went bam, bam, bam. "How *dare* you come running through this school making all that mess in the corridor!"

"And in the hall," said Mr Bannister, "that's just been polished."

Josie Smith looked at the floor where she'd come in. There was a trail of mud and petals and bits of grass and hen food. Then she looked at her roses. There were no roses left, only the stalks with fuzzy brown lumps on the end of them.

"Excuse me, Miss Valentine," shouted Miss Potts to the new teacher, and she marched in and got hold of Josie Smith's shoulder so hard that it hurt.

"What's your mother thinking of," she roared, "sending you to school at this time and in this state? You're wet through! Where's your coat?"

Josie Smith didn't know.

"Doesn't your mother know any better than to send you out without a coat in this weather? Blow your nose!"

Josie Smith felt in the pocket of her kilt but her handkerchief wasn't there.

"Where's your handkerchief?" roared Miss Potts.

Josie Smith didn't know.

"And what's all that rubbish in your

hands?" roared Miss Potts. "Throw it in the wastepaper basket!"

Josie Smith went and threw the stalks in the wastepaper basket.

"All over my floor," said Mr Bannister.

"Come back here," roared Miss Potts, "and show me your hands!"

Josie Smith showed her muddy hands.

"Go and wash them!" roared Miss Potts, "and your face! And take those filthy wellingtons off and put your gym shoes on!"

Josie Smith went.

When she came back, Miss Potts was still shouting. She was mad at everybody now.

"And if any child comes in late again there'll be trouble! Gary Grimes, blow your nose! I've told you all, time and time again, to bring a handkerchief to school! And don't let me hear of any books being torn again in this class or I'll have your parents in! Thank you, Miss Valentine!"

And she marched out. Mr Bannister went out behind her with his brush.

Josie Smith stood where she was and her

chest was going bam, bam, bam, but she was too frightened to cry. She was too frightened to look at the new teacher but she looked at her desk and saw Eileen's present in its box and a bunch of flowers in a vase and three apples. She wondered where her apple was, but she couldn't remember. Then the new teacher said quietly, "Go to your place."

Josie Smith went to her table and sat down with Eileen and Gary Grimes and Rawley Baxter. They had to do sums. Josie Smith couldn't do sums. She tried as hard as she could but she couldn't do three take away seven no matter how hard she tried, so when she couldn't try any more she took the three away from the seven and got four. Then she smelt the new teacher's perfume and a hand with shiny pink nails pointed at the sum in her book.

"You've copied them all down wrongly," the new teacher's voice said. "You should have added up, not taken away."

At playtime it was still raining and they had to stay in. Everybody was noisy and fed up and Josie Smith felt tired. Afterwards, she had to do all her sums again when the others were all drawing dinosaurs. Then it was dinner time. Josie Smith didn't like her dinner. It smelt horrible and there were lumps in it and she'd forgotten to bring a paper bag in her pocket to hide them in. When she couldn't eat the lumps the dinner lady shouted. Eileen was horrible as well because she wasn't friends with Josie Smith. School was horrible all day. In the afternoon they had to write a story but Josie Smith couldn't remember any of the stories she'd made up in bed and as soon as she started writing she went crooked and then made a mistake. She couldn't borrow Eileen's pencil with a rubber on the end because they weren't friends, so she rubbed out with her finger and made a hole in the page. Josie Smith wanted to go home. When it was time she ran all the way home by herself and in at her own front door.

"Where's your coat?" asked Josie's mum, stopping her sewing machine. "You're wet through! Where's your coat?"

"Atchoo!" said Josie Smith. "Atchoo!"

"Oh, for goodness' sake," said Josie's mum. "You'll have tonsillitis again, next news. Come on, straight to bed."

Josie Smith went straight to bed and her mum brought her something to eat on a tray and said, "You'd better stay in bed tomorrow, just in case."

"Atchoo!" said Josie Smith. "Atchoo!"

Ginger stood up in his basket and stared at her.

"Will Ginger catch my cold?" asked Josie Smith.

"No," said Josie's mum.

"I'm glad I'm not going to school tomorrow," said Josie Smith. "I don't like it any more."

"Why not?" asked Josie's mum. "You haven't been getting in trouble, have you?"

"No," said Josie Smith with her eyes shut.

"Well, why don't you want to go, then? Something must have happened."

"Eileen wouldn't lend me her pencil with a rubber on the end," said Josie Smith, "and I had to rub out with my finger and it made a hole."

"Is that all?" said Josie's mum.

"And I didn't like my dinner," said Josie Smith.

And then they said Goodnight.

The next morning it was raining again and Josie Smith stayed in bed. She heard the milkman come and she heard Eileen come and call for her and then go away again. She heard all the children going past to school and running and shouting in the yard far away. Then she fell asleep again. After dinner, Josie's mum said she could get dressed and come down and crayon by the fire. Josie Smith came down. She sat by the fire with her crayons and crayoning book and sometimes she listened to the rain pattering on the window and sometimes she listened to her mum's sewing machine going Tr-r-r-r-r-r-r-ik, tr-r-r-r-r-r-ik, tr-r-r-r-r-r-ik.

Then her mum said, "I'd better run across to Mrs Chadwick's and get something for tea."

"Can I come?" said Josie Smith.

"No," said Josie's mum. "It's raining. You can watch me from the window."

So Josie Smith climbed on the chair by the window and watched her mum run across the street in the rain and go in Mrs Chadwick's shop. Then she saw Mrs Scowcroft. Mrs Scowcroft went in Mrs Chadwick's shop too, and she had Josie Smith's coat over her arm. Josie Smith jumped down from the chair so that Mrs Scowcroft wouldn't see her. She remembered that she'd been in Mr Scowcroft's allotment when he wasn't there, and in his hen shed, and left her coat and been late for school. If Mrs Scowcroft told over her she would get shouted at; she might get smacked. Josie Smith sat down on the rug. She didn't want to look out the window any more. Then the door went Bam! and her mum came in. Josie Smith put her head down and looked at her crayoning book.

"Well!" said Josie's mum. "I've been hearing some stories about you! Look what I've got here."

But Josie Smith didn't look because she knew it was her coat.

"I left it at Mr Scowcroft's," she said.

"Look!" said Josie's mum.

Josie Smith looked. It wasn't her coat. It was a bunch of pom-pom dahlias. "Mrs Scowcroft brought them for you, as well as your coat, to say thank you. Mr Scowcroft's got bronchitis and she had to go and feed the hens for him yesterday. But when she got there somebody had fed them."

"Yes," said Josie Smith, and then she said, "I dug as well."

"And weren't you late for school?" asked Josie's mum.

"Yes," said Josie Smith.

"And is that why you were upset?" asked Josie's mum.

"I don't know," said Josie Smith. Then she said, "Can I take the pom-pom dahlias to school?"

"If you like," said Josie's mum. "Why don't you write a little story to take as well?"

"All right," said Josie Smith.

So Josie Smith wrote a story by the fire and then she went to bed early. The next day, when Eileen came to call for her she was ready with a ribbon in her hair and her story and the bunch of pom-pom dahlias and a note to say she'd been ill.

"What beautiful flowers," Miss Valentine said. "Are you better now?"

"Yes," said Josie Smith.

"And will you get all your sums right today?"

"Yes," said Josie Smith, shutting her eyes tight because it was a lie.

"It's a shame you were away yesterday," Miss Valentine said, "because everybody wrote a story and there's going to be a prize for the best one."

"I wrote a story," said Josie Smith, "with a giant and some gypsies and a witch in it." And she gave her story to Miss Valentine.

Josie Smith liked school today. Miss Valentine helped her with her sums and Eileen lent her her pencil to rub out with and they had chips for dinner.

When it was nearly home time, Miss Valentine said, "Everybody come and sit round me." Everybody went. Then she said, "Josie Smith, stand up."

Josie Smith stood up.

"Josie Smith wins the prize for the best story," Miss Valentine said.

"Josie Smith's always the best in the class at stories," Eileen said.

"And she's going to learn to be just as good at sums," Miss Valentine said. "Isn't that right, Josie?"

"Yes," said Josie Smith, shutting her eyes because it was a lie.

"Here you are," Miss Valentine said.

Josie Smith opened her eyes. Then she opened them wider. Then she smiled a big smile and got hold tight of her prize. A shiny, stripy, brand-new, sharpened pencil, with a rubber on the end.

Boffy and the Teacher Eater

Margaret Stuart-Barry

Boffy was six years old. He was small and rather thin. Large spectacles covered his pale, serious face. Boffy did not think about tadpoles and chewing-gum and model cars the way other boys did, he wanted more than anything to be an inventor.

"You can't be one until you're grown up," said his tall, important-looking father. "You're not old enough."

"But I'm a genius," pointed out Boffy.

"Yes," said his mother, whose name was Mrs Smith, "I'm afraid he is."

She found living with a genius very

difficult; geniuses are inclined to think it's tea-time when it's only breakfast-time. And they make complicated arrangements with the biscuits instead of just eating them. And *always* use a long word where a short one would do.

Mr Smith was going to work. He was rushing to catch the underground train. Boffy had made a wonderful vehicle out of empty fruit cans. It hopped on and off pavements, knew when not to bump into lamp-posts without being told, and could even climb over things if necessary, like a great caterpillar.

"Borrow it," suggested Boffy. "It will get you there more quickly."

"No, thank you," said Mr Smith politely. He preferred the more conventional form of transport.

So Boffy climbed into the fruit-can vehicle himself, and rattled off to town to collect his mother's groceries. He loaded beans into one container, potatoes into another, and secured half a boiled pig to the back. He took longer doing that than he had expected, so when he came to the gas-works he drove straight over it instead of going round it, which saved a lot of time. This greatly surprised Constable Scuffer. But by the time he'd thought what to do about it Boffy was out of sight.

Mrs Smith was glad to have her groceries so quickly. She wanted to get the lunch in the oven early so that she could make a start with her spring-cleaning.

Soon the kitchen was full of buckets and mops and soap and polish and dusters and dishcloths.

"Did you ever see such dust!" she exclaimed. She was red in the face and quite bothered.

"I'll help you," said Boffy.

"No, thank you," panted Mrs Smith; she was aghast at the thought of another of Boffy's inventions.

"There must be quicker ways of cleaning a room than this!" Boffy waved his hand at the conglomeration of mops and dusters.

"There is no better way than by getting

down on one's hands and knees," answered his mother, beginning to do just that.

But Boffy was already in his little workshop behind the cabbage patch. He knew exactly what he was going to do because, as I have told you, he was a genius. In no time at all he had made a large interesting-looking machine. It had a horn at one end, and a plastic sack at the other, and it was held together by a great many rubber tubes.

"What is it?" asked Mrs Smith, as Boffy appeared in the kitchen doorway with the new invention.

"It's a Dust Extractor, of course."

"Well, I don't need it." His mother was quite firm. "I've been doing my spring-cleaning this way for a good many years now, and I don't intend to change."

"Yes, but look how long it takes you." Before Mrs Smith could stop him, he had switched on the Dust Extractor.

"It works!" cheered Boffy.

I cannot describe the noise that followed – like a percussion band, but noisier! Anyway, it drowned Mrs Smith's screams of "Stop! Stop!"

Brooms and mops rattled up into the Dust Extractor. A jar of marmalade flew off the table, followed by cups and saucers and the tablecloth. Boffy was delighted. Not *all* his inventions worked. This one was doing fine. He moved it closer to the cooker, which looked exceptionally dusty. At once the pans came to life. Off flew the lids and out popped the potatoes and the runner beans. They

slithered and bumped down the tubes of the Dust Extractor. They took the boiling water with them and carried on cooking merrily inside the plastic bag. Last of all the oven door swung open and out shot the half pig.

Mrs Smith was completely DISTRAUGHT.

"You are a DISGRACE!" thundered Boffy's father when he came home for lunch (which was now only a buttered biscuit and a cup of tea). "You will go straight to your room, without lunch, without afternoon tea, and without supper, and you will *stay* there. And while you are there you will rid your head of all nonsensical ideas."

"I'm sorry, Father," apologized Boffy. And he polished his spectacles on his shirt.

It was hard being so awfully clever.

For a whole week Boffy behaved like a model boy – more or less. He sat in the garden and counted the bees. When he had counted five hundred and sixty-nine he thought of a number and divided them by it. Then he counted earwigs and subtracted them from the number of leaves on the mulberry bush.

When the dustbin-lorry arrived he carted his Dust Extractor round to the front garden and offered it to the dustbin-men. At first they did not want to take it, but when they saw how it operated they said, "Thank you very much. This will make our job a whole lot easier."

And they took it away.

Mr and Mrs Smith didn't know themselves, it was so quiet around the place. Mrs Smith was worried.

"Do you think you ought to have been *quite* so severe with Boffy?" she wondered.

"Well, perhaps not," answered her husband. "But we can't have these frightful inventions of his upsetting the whole household." (He was a little worried himself.)

"If he could invent something small – like a Boiled-egg Opener or . . . or . . . a . . ." But Mrs Smith hadn't any more ideas.

"I'll speak to him," decided Mr Smith quite kindly. "Boffy," he shouted down the garden, "just be more careful in future, that's all."

"Yes, Father," answered Boffy. He was relieved.

The following day was a school day. Boffy was in Class IV – on account of his being so clever, that is. He should have been in Class I, but the teacher in that room couldn't cope with him. He was constantly correcting her, and she didn't like that at all. Mr Grim, however, had been to a university, so he knew one or two things Boffy didn't.

Today he was in a bad mood, because it was the first day back after a holiday. He stared at the class ferociously and made Jenny Jenny cry. He threw a new piece of chalk at Herbert Entwhistle, and made them all write lines.

"He's horrible, *horrible*," wept Jenny Jenny.

"Don't cry, Jenny Jenny," comforted Boffy. "I have an idea. Tomorrow you will have nothing to worry about."

After tea he retired to his shed behind the cabbage patch and he thought, and he banged and he screwed and he fixed. Then he locked up, kissed his parents good night, and went to bed early. His small head was quite worn out.

Next morning Boffy collected his new invention from the shed and set off for school. He carried it a long way round down the back streets, just in case he should meet any of his important-looking father's important-looking friends. But he met a milkman, and Mr Leggit, the postman, and that was all.

The school cloakroom was packed with children when Boffy appeared in the doorway with his latest invention.

"Oooh, what's that?" asked the children, gathering round.

"It's a Teacher Eater," explained Boffy.

"Do you mean it actually *eats* teachers?" asked the incredulous children.

"Of course it does," replied Boffy. "That's what I've just told you."

The Teacher Eater was very large. It was a cross between a robot and a dragon. It was constructed chiefly of tin and had a huge jagged jaw like the blade of a saw. On its face, which was simply enormous, Boffy had painted a big pleasant smile. This was not strictly necessary to the functioning of the machine, but Boffy did not want to frighten Jenny Jenny. He had even troubled to glue a black wig on to the Teacher Eater's head.

"Oooh, I like him!" said Jenny Jenny. "He's *super*, Boffy!"

Boffy kept the Teacher Eater hidden under a pile of coats until after play, then he wheeled it out into Class I. The Teacher Eater trundled across the classroom floor and completely devoured the Infants' teacher.

"Hurray!" cheered the children.

The uproar brought the other teachers racing out of their rooms. They clapped their hands and shouted angry commands. The Teacher Eater didn't like that; it trundled more quickly towards them. A crowd of children skipped and jumped behind it. Suddenly it fancied the Art teacher. She was a delectable mouthful. Her scarlet stockings were the last the children saw of her.

"*Mon dieu!*" gasped the French master. He had no time to say more.

The terrible machine rolled down the corridor hungry for more. It found the

Mathematics teachers rather difficult to digest: numbers and question marks shot out of its ears all over the place.

The Teacher Eater was thoroughly enjoying eating teachers. It charged hither and thither gulping them down whole until at last there was not a single one left.

Boffy stored his invention in the games cupboard and locked the door.

"Well, children," commanded Boffy, "back to your classrooms, and I shall be round presently."

No one contradicted. They did as they were told. They were quite content to look upon Boffy as their new Headmaster.

Boffy retired to the Headmaster's room to draw up a new timetable. It consisted chiefly of games and do-as-you-like lessons. The children played games until they were exhausted. In the do-as-you-like lessons most of them went home.

It was not long before every parent was frantically phoning every other parent. The whole town was ringing and buzzing. Mr and Mrs Smith were thoroughly alarmed and more than a little annoyed with their son.

"You are a DISGRACE!" (again) thundered Mr Smith, "and you will go straight to your room, without tea, without supper, and without breakfast, and you will *stay* there. And whilst you are there you will consider the damage you have done."

The school governors sat up very late that night discussing hard and partaking of refreshments. They were very annoyed indeed. The sort of problems they were used to dealing with were problems like whether to buy a heated fish-tank, or whether to buy new desks for the Infants. They had never had to deal with a problem like the Teacher Eater. It was all extremely irritating. They decided to visit the school at nine o'clock sharp the following morning. Five minutes later they decided they wouldn't, as the machine which ate teachers might very well turn out to be a School Governor Eater too!

"Highly probable, highly probable," they muttered wisely.

The next day all the children were in school very early. They wanted to see what Boffy had in store for them. They expected that the morning would be spent in playing games, and the afternoon in painting or in general messing around. But Boffy had been considering the matter. He was enjoying being a Headmaster, and he had decided that his pupils should get down to some serious work. He pinned up a large notice in the hall. It read:

1st lesson – Maths
2nd lesson – Greek
3rd lesson – Chemistry
4th lesson – Lecture in the assembly
        hall on "The Origin of the
        Species", given by Boffy.
(Signed) Boffy (*Headmaster*)

"What about play-time?" complained Simon
Goodbody halfway through the morning.

"You had enough play yesterday," scolded
Boffy sternly.

"But *you're* not working," persisted Simon
sulkily. "You're just sitting in the Headmaster's room doing nothing."

"Of course. That's what Headmasters *do*.
You will stay in after school and write 'I must
not be bold' one hundred times."

Simon hated that. But Boffy sounded so
much like a real Headmaster that he was
afraid to disobey.

Then a *catastrophe* happened. The Dinner
Lady did not appear. She had heard all about
the dreadful Teacher Eater and was terrified

out of her wits. She was afraid it might turn nasty and become a Dinner Lady Eater too. And so the children had no dinner. Jenny Jenny began to cry.

"I'm hungry, Boffy," she wailed. "Ever so hungry."

"So am I," said Johnny and Kate, the twins. And they began to cry also.

Soon the whole school was wailing and moaning.

"And your lessons are too hard," gulped Jenny Jenny, quite heartbroken, "and I can't do them."

"Neither can I," sobbed all the others together.

"I wish our teacher was back," sniffled Jenny Jenny, "I wish she *was*."

Boffy was cross (and worried and a bit sorry).

"One just can't please some folks," he grunted.

At that moment, the school door opened and in stamped Mr Smith looking specially important.

"Now then! Now then!" he bellowed. "This nonsense has gone on quite long enough. Where is the Teacher Eater, Boffy?"

Obediently Boffy unlocked the games cupboard, and there was the Teacher Eater, gleaming in the electric light.

"Right," said Mr Smith, pulling it out. "Now *I* have brought along an invention. It's not a new one, and it's not a big one, but it works. Your mother lent it to me."

It was a tin-opener. Mr Smith started to use it and cut out a large hole in the Teacher Eater's back.

Out rolled the Infants' teacher, then the Art mistress, followed by the Maths master, the French master, and one or two others, and finally the Headmaster himself. They sat in a heap on the floor, looking dazed and very crumpled. They could not think where they had been or why. Then they caught sight of the Teacher Eater and remembered. The Headmaster turned very pale indeed, then he said, "There will be a half-day's holiday today. Good afternoon, children."

When Mr Smith had driven his son home he said, "You are a DISGRACE! (third time) and you will go straight to your room—"

"—without tea, without supper, and without breakfast," finished Boffy for him. "And I will consider the damage I have done, and I will *never* invent anything again – not until I'm grown up anyway."

Then Mr Smith laughed very loudly, and Mrs Smith laughed too. And they thought how lucky they were after all to have a genius in the family.

And all the other mothers and fathers in the town thought how lucky *they* were that they hadn't.

Cyclone

Sita Heti

Talofa lava. You know a little while ago when I was in the same class as you I hated going to school? Do you want to know why? Well, I'll tell you.

Everyday when it was roll call, my teacher, Mrs Brown, called everyone's name out, no trouble. But, when it came to my name she suddenly got tongue-tied. As soon as she opened her mouth to speak, I felt sick because I knew what lay ahead. When she said my name, it made all the other kids crack up laughing. Their laughter sounded like broken glass, you know, sharp and painful.

I was so ashamed of my name. Sometimes I would get so mad I would just get up and run out of class. But this only made things worse because when I went back, all the other kids would tease me more about being a sooky.

I always wished that I could have an ordinary name like Jane or Susan. Why did I have to be the odd one out? Why did I have to be the one with the funny name? Why did I have to be the one that all the kids laughed at?

I hated my name so much that I told everyone not to call me it. I said that my mother had changed my name to Mary. It made no difference. Mrs Brown still tried to say my whole name, last name and all.

Sometimes it was all too much for me, so I sat at the back so I could lift up my desk lid to wipe away the tears.

Each morning I would act sick so that my mum would keep me home from school. But she would always send me off, just in time for roll call, the worst part of my day. I couldn't wait until my favourite part of the day, home time.

One day Mrs Brown was away and we had a

relieving teacher called Mrs Siaosi. She was nice. She looked like Aunty Nese back in Samoa. She had long brown hair tied in a bun, and a great big smile. The thing that reminded me most of my aunty was the flower in her hair. I liked her a lot.

When she took out the roll, I felt funny. I was scared. I thought that she would say my name wrong just like all the other teachers. When she came closer to my name, I sat with my mouth open and I was breathing hard. I could feel my heart beating fast. Then I heard her say my name. It sounded like my mother calling me. When she said my name right, it felt so good. I had never heard a teacher say my name like that before. I was so happy that I jumped out of my seat and yelled, "Yes, that's me, here I am!" and that made all the other kids look at me but I didn't care. I just felt so good. I wanted to shout my name out loud so everyone would remember it.

All day when she spoke to me or called out to me, I would run to her and say, "Yes, that's me! Here I am!" She must have thought I was crazy or something.

After school I ran home to tell my mum about my wonderful new teacher. My mum was so happy that I'd had a good day for once that she came to school with me the next day. She went to the staffroom to see Mrs Siaosi. As soon as they met, they started talking in Samoan, laughing and joking like old friends.

I heard the bell go so I had to hurry to class. I wished that it was Mrs Siaosi teaching me instead of Mrs Brown. I didn't feel like being made fun of this morning so I stayed outside

the classroom until Mrs Brown finished the roll. Then I heard a voice say, "Saikoloni, what are you doing out here? You should be inside with your class."

I turned around slowly to find Mrs Siaosi looking at me. "Please don't make me go in there today. They all hate me and I hate them. They laugh at me at roll call because Mrs Brown doesn't know how to say my stupid name properly and they tease me for the rest of the day. I just wish that I hadn't been named Saikoloni . . ."

I stopped. I could see that what I'd said had made Mrs Siaosi angry.

"Now look here, girl, you come from Samoa and you know that most of the kids in your class are Palagi. They do not know better. You must make them understand. Do you know what your name means?" she said to me while I tried to calm down.

"No," I said quietly.

"Your mother told me that you were born during a big storm, a cyclone, in Samoa. You were dedicated to your uncle and cousins who died in the cyclone. You are the memory of them and you should always be proud of it. Hold your head up to show people that you are proud to know where you come from and why you're here. Besides, Saikoloni is better than plain Jane or ordinary Susan. It's special. There are many of them, but only one of you. Now you go inside and you explain to your class what your name means and why you have it. And don't forget to tell them how to say it."

With that she opened the door to my class-room and led me inside. The first thing I heard was, "Hey, look! Lony-stony-pony's here."

The whole class started laughing. I was so embarrassed my face felt like it was burning. But then my embarrassment turned into something else. I don't know what it was, but it made me go to the front of the classroom. My mouth opened, and I heard myself say, "My name is Saikoloni Tapumuulietoa, and I come from a village called Patamea, in Savai'i in Samoa. It is beautiful over there: lots of coconuts to eat and lots of beaches to swim at. When we came over here, we had to buy everything we ate, and we are so far from the water.

"In English my name means 'Cyclone', which is a big storm like the one that hit Samoa in 1990. My mother named me this to remember my uncle and my cousins who died in a storm when I was born."

When I had finished all this, I took a deep breath. I thought for sure that Mrs Brown was going to growl at me. When I looked up at her, she smiled and told me that she'd thought she was saying my name right. She said I shouldn't have been scared to tell her about it.

After that, school got a lot better, and I have Mrs Siaosi to thank for that. So if your teacher is not saying your name right, don't make the same mistake I did. Just have the heart to stand up and say, "Excuse me, but that's not how you say my name," and explain how it should be said. You are most important and your name is your parents' present to you, so don't ever regret having it.

Tofa soifua.

Ramona's Great Day

Beverly Cleary

"**I** am *not* a pest," Ramona Quimby told her big sister Beezus.

"Then stop acting like a pest," said Beezus, whose real name was Beatrice. She was standing by the front window waiting for her friend Mary Jane to walk to school with her.

"I'm not acting like a pest. I'm singing and skipping," said Ramona, who had only recently learnt to skip with both feet. Ramona did not think she was a pest. No matter what others said, she never thought she was a pest. The people who called her a pest were always bigger and so they could be unfair.

Ramona went on with her singing and

skipping. "This is a great day, a great day, a great day!" she sang, and to Ramona, who was feeling grown up in a dress instead of play clothes, this was a great day, the greatest day of her whole life. No longer would she have to sit on her tricycle watching Beezus and Henry Huggins and the rest of the boys and girls in the neighbourhood go off to school. Today she was going to school too. Today she was going to learn to read and write and do all the things that would help her catch up with Beezus.

"Come *on*, Mama!" urged Ramona, pausing in her singing and skipping. "We don't want to be late for school."

"Don't pester, Ramona," said Mrs Quimby. "I'll get you there in plenty of time."

"I'm *not* pestering," protested Ramona, who never meant to pester. She was not a slowcoach grown-up. She was a girl who could not wait. Life was so interesting she had to find out what happened next.

Then Mary Jane arrived. "Mrs Quimby, would it be all right if Beezus and I take

Ramona to kindergarten?" she asked.

"No!" said Ramona instantly. Mary Jane was one of those girls who always wanted to pretend she was a mother and who always wanted Ramona to be the baby. Nobody was going to catch Ramona being a baby on her first day of school.

"Why not?" Mrs Quimby asked of Ramona. "You could walk to school with Beezus and Mary Jane just like a big girl."

"No, I couldn't." Ramona was not fooled for an instant. Mary Jane would talk in that silly voice she used when she was being a mother and take her by the hand and help her across the street, and everyone would think she really was a baby.

"Please, Ramona," coaxed Beezus. "It would be lots of fun to take you in and introduce you to the kindergarten teacher."

"No!" said Ramona, and stamped her foot. Beezus and Mary Jane might have fun, but she wouldn't. Nobody but a genuine grown-up was going to take her to school. If she had to, she would make a great big noisy fuss, and when Ramona made a great big noisy fuss, she usually got her own way. Great big noisy fusses were often necessary when a girl was the youngest member of the family and the youngest person on her block.

"All right, Ramona," said Mrs Quimby. "Don't make a great big noisy fuss. If that's the way you feel about it, you don't have to walk with the girls. I'll take you."

"Hurry, Mama," said Ramona happily, as she watched Beezus and Mary Jane go out of the door. But when Ramona finally got her mother out of the house, she was disappointed to see one of her mother's friends, Mrs Kemp, approaching with her son Howie and his little sister Willa Jean, who was riding in a stroller. "Hurry, Mama," urged Ramona, not wanting to wait for the Kemps. Because their mothers were friends, she and Howie were expected to get along with one another.

"Hi there!" Mrs Kemp called out, so of course Ramona's mother had to wait.

Howie stared at Ramona. He did not like

having to get along with her any more than she liked having to get along with him.

Ramona stared back. Howie was a solid-looking boy with curly blond hair. ("Such a waste on a boy," his mother often remarked.) The legs of his new jeans were turned up, and he was wearing a new shirt with long sleeves. He did not look the least bit excited about starting kindergarten. That was the trouble with Howie, Ramona felt. He never got excited. Straight-haired Willa Jean, who was interesting to Ramona because she was so sloppy, blew out a mouthful of wet crumbs and laughed at her cleverness.

"Today my baby leaves me," remarked Mrs Quimby with a smile, as the little group proceeded down Klickitat Street towards Glenwood School.

Ramona, who enjoyed being her mother's baby, did not enjoy being called her mother's baby, especially in front of Howie.

"They grow up quickly," observed Mrs Kemp.

Ramona could not understand why grown-ups always talked about how quickly children grew up. Ramona thought growing up was the slowest thing there was, slower even than waiting for Christmas to come. She had been waiting years just to get to kindergarten, and the last half hour was the slowest part of all.

When the group reached the intersection nearest Glenwood School, Ramona was pleased to see that Beezus's friend Henry Huggins was the traffic boy in charge of that particular corner. After Henry had led them across the street, Ramona ran off towards the kindergarten, which was a temporary building with its own playground. Mothers and children were already entering the open door. Some of the children looked frightened, and one girl was crying.

"We're late!" cried Ramona. "Hurry!"

Howie was not a boy to be hurried. "I don't see any tricycles," he said critically. "I don't see any dirt to dig in."

Ramona was scornful. "This isn't nursery school. Tricycles and dirt are for nursery school." Her own tricycle was hidden in the garage, because it was too babyish for her now that she was going to school.

Some big first-grade boys ran past yelling, "Kindergarten babies! Kindergarten babies!"

"We are *not* babies!" Ramona yelled back, as she led her mother into the kindergarten. Once inside she stayed close to her. Everything was so strange, and there was so much to see: the little tables and chairs; the row of cupboards, each with a different picture on the door; the play stove; and the wooden blocks big enough to stand on.

The teacher, who was new to Glenwood School, turned out to be so young and pretty she could not have been a grown-up very long. It was rumoured she had never taught at school before. "Hello, Ramona. My name is Miss Binney," she said, speaking each syllable distinctly as she pinned Ramona's name to her dress. "I am so glad you have come to kindergarten." Then she took Ramona by the hand and led her to one of the little tables and chairs. "Sit here for the present," she said with a smile.

A present! thought Ramona, and knew at once she was going to like Miss Binney.

"Goodbye, Ramona," said Mrs Quimby. "Be a good girl."

As she watched her mother walk out of the door, Ramona decided school was going to be even better than she had hoped. Nobody had told her she was going to get a present the very first day. What kind of present could it be, she wondered, trying to remember if Beezus had ever been given a present by her teacher.

Ramona listened carefully while Miss Binney showed Howie to a table, but all her teacher said was, "Howie, I would like you to sit here." Well! thought Ramona. Not everyone is going to get a present so Miss Binney must like me best. Ramona watched and listened as the other boys and girls arrived, but Miss Binney did not tell anyone else he was going to get a present if he sat in a certain chair. Ramona wondered if her present would be wrapped in fancy paper and tied with a ribbon like a birthday present. She hoped so.

As Ramona sat waiting for her present she watched the other children being introduced to Miss Binney by their mothers. She found two members of the morning kindergarten especially interesting. One was a boy named Davy, who was small, thin and eager. He was the only boy in the class in short trousers, and Ramona liked him at once. She liked him so much she decided she would like to kiss him.

The other interesting person was a big girl named Susan. Susan's hair looked like the hair on the girls in the pictures of the old-fashioned stories Beezus liked to read. It was reddish-brown and hung in curls like springs that touched her shoulders and bounced as she walked. Ramona had never seen such curls before. All the curly-haired girls she knew wore their hair short. Ramona put her hand to her own short straight hair, which was an ordinary brown, and longed to touch that bright springy hair. She longed to stretch one of those curls and watch it spring back. *Boing*! thought Ramona, making a mental noise like a spring on a television cartoon and wishing for thick, springy *boing-boing* hair like Susan's.

Howie interrupted Ramona's admiration of Susan's hair. "How soon do you think we get to go out and play?" he asked.

"Maybe after Miss Binney gives me the present," Ramona answered. "She said she was going to give me one."

"How come she's going to give you a present?" Howie wanted to know. "She didn't say anything about giving me a present."

"Maybe she likes me best," said Ramona.

This news did not make Howie happy. He turned to the next boy, and said, "*She*'s going to get a present."

Ramona wondered how long she would have to sit there to get the present. If only Miss Binney understood how hard waiting was for her! When the last child had been welcomed and the last tearful mother had departed, Miss Binney gave a little talk about the rule of the kindergarten and showed the class the door that led to the bathroom. Next she assigned each person a little cupboard. Ramona's cupboard had a picture of a yellow duck on the door, and Howie's had a green frog. Miss Binney explained that their hooks in the cloakroom were marked with the same pictures. Then she asked the class to follow her quietly into the cloakroom to find their hooks.

Difficult though waiting was for her, Ramona did not budge. Miss Binney had not told her to get up and go into the cloakroom for her present. She had told her to sit for the present, and Ramona was going to sit until she got it. She would sit as if she were glued to the chair.

Howie scowled at Ramona as he returned from the cloakroom, and said to another boy, "The teacher is going to give *her* a present."

Naturally the boy wanted to know why. "I don't know," admitted Ramona. "She told me that if I sat here I would get a present. I guess she likes me best."

By the time Miss Binney returned from the cloakroom, word had spread around the classroom that Ramona was going to get a present.

Next Miss Binney taught the class the words of a puzzling song about "the dawnzer lee light", which Ramona did not understand because she did not know what a dawnzer was. "Oh, say, can you see by the dawnzer lee light," sang Miss Binney, and Ramona decided that a dawnzer was another word for a lamp.

When Miss Binney had gone over the song several times, she asked the class to stand and sing it with her. Ramona did not budge. Neither did Howie and some of the others, and Ramona knew they were hoping for a present too. Copycats, she thought.

"Stand up straight like good Americans," said Miss Binney so firmly that Howie and the others reluctantly stood up.

Ramona decided she would have to be a good American sitting down.

"Ramona," said Miss Binney, "aren't you going to stand with the rest of us?"

Ramona thought quickly. Maybe the question was some kind of test, like a test in a fairy tale. Maybe Miss Binney was testing her to see if she could get her out of her seat. If she failed the test, she would not get the present.

"I can't," said Ramona.

Miss Binney looked puzzled, but she did not insist that Ramona stand while she led the class through the dawnzer song. Ramona sang along with the others and hoped that her present came next, but when the song ended, Miss Binney made no mention of the present. Instead she picked up a book. Ramona decided that at last the time had come to learn to read.

Miss Binney stood in front of her class and began to read aloud from *Mike Mulligan and his Steam Shovel*, a book that was a favourite of Ramona's because, unlike so many books for her age, it was neither quiet and sleepy nor sweet and pretty. Ramona, pretending she was glued to her chair, enjoyed hearing the story again and listened quietly with the rest of the kindergarten to the story of Mike Mulligan's old-fashioned steam shovel, which proved its worth by digging the basement for the new town hall of Poppersville in a single day beginning at dawn and ending as the sun went down.

As Ramona listened a question came into her mind, a question that had often puzzled her about the books that were read to her. Somehow books always left out one of the most important things anyone would want to know. Now that Ramona was in school, and school was a place for learning, perhaps

Miss Binney could answer the question. Ramona waited quietly until her teacher had finished the story, and then she raised her hand the way Miss Binney had told the class they should raise their hands when they wanted to speak in school.

Joey, who did not remember to raise his hand, spoke out. "That's a good book."

Miss Binney smiled at Ramona, and said, "I like the way Ramona remembers to raise her hand when she has something to say. Yes, Ramona?"

Ramona's hopes soared. Her teacher had smiled at her. "Miss Binney, I want to know – how did Mike Mulligan go to the bathroom when he was digging the basement of the town hall?"

Miss Binney's smile seemed to last longer than smiles usually last. Ramona glanced uneasily around and saw that others were waiting with interest for the answer. Everybody wanted to know how Mike Mulligan went to the bathroom.

"Well—" said Miss Binney at last. "I don't

really know, Ramona. The book doesn't tell us."

"I always wanted to know too," said Howie, without raising his hand, and others murmured in agreement. The whole class, it seemed, had been wondering how Mike Mulligan went to the bathroom.

"Maybe he stopped the steam shovel and climbed out of the hole he was digging and went to a service station," suggested a boy named Eric.

"He couldn't. The book says he had to work as fast as he could all day," Howie pointed out. "It doesn't say he stopped."

Miss Binney faced the twenty-nine earnest members of the kindergarten, all of whom wanted to know how Mike Mulligan went to the bathroom.

"Boys and girls," she began, and spoke in her clear, distinct way. "The reason the book does not tell us how Mike Mulligan went to the bathroom is that it is not an important part of the story. The story is about digging the basement of the town hall, and that is what the book tells us."

Miss Binney spoke as if this explanation ended the matter, but the kindergarten was not convinced. Ramona knew and the rest of the class knew that knowing how to go to the bathroom *was* important. They were surprised that Miss Binney did not understand, because she had showed them the bathroom the very first thing. Ramona could see there were some things she was not going to learn in school, and along with the rest of the class she stared reproachfully at Miss Binney.

The teacher looked embarrassed, as if she knew she had disappointed her kindergarten. She recovered quickly, closed the book and told the class that if they would walk quietly out to the playground she would teach them a game called Grey Duck.

Ramona did not budge. She watched the rest of the class leave the room and admired Susan's *boing-boing* curls as they bounced about her shoulders, but she did not stir from her seat. Only Miss Binney could unstick the imaginary glue that held her there.

"Don't you want to learn to play Grey Duck, Ramona?" Miss Binney asked.

Ramona nodded. "Yes, but I can't."

"Why not?" asked Miss Binney.

"I can't leave my seat," said Ramona. When Miss Binney looked blank, she added, "Because of the present."

"What present?" Miss Binney seemed so genuinely puzzled that Ramona became uneasy. The teacher sat down in the little chair next to Ramona's, and said, "Tell me why you can't play Grey Duck."

Ramona squirmed, worn out with waiting. She had an uneasy feeling that something had gone wrong someplace. "I want to play Grey Duck, but you—" she stopped, feeling that she might be about to say the wrong thing.

"But I what?" asked Miss Binney.

"Well . . . uh . . . you said if I sat here I would get a present," said Ramona at last, "but you didn't say how long I had to sit here."

If Miss Binney looked puzzled before, she

now looked baffled. "Ramona, I don't
understand—" she began.

"Yes, you did," said Ramona, nodding. "You
told me to sit here for the present, and I have
been sitting here ever since school started
and you haven't given me a present."

Miss Binney's face turned red and she
looked so embarrassed that Ramona felt
completely confused. Teachers were not
supposed to look that way.

Miss Binney spoke gently. "Ramona, I'm
afraid we've had a misunderstanding."

Ramona was blunt. "You mean I don't get a present?"

"I'm afraid not," admitted Miss Binney. "You see 'for the present' means for now. I meant that I wanted you to sit here for now, because later I may have the children sit at different desks."

"Oh." Ramona was so disappointed she had nothing to say. Words were so puzzling. *Present* should mean a present just as *attack* should mean to stick tacks in people.

By now all the children were crowding around the door to see what had happened to their teacher. "I'm so sorry," said Miss Binney. "It's all my fault. I should have used different words."

"That's all right," said Ramona, ashamed to have the class see that she was not going to get a present after all.

"All right, class," said Miss Binney briskly. "Let's go outside and play Grey Duck. You too, Ramona."

Grey Duck turned out to be an easy game, and Ramona's spirits recovered quickly from her disappointment. The class formed a circle, and the person who was "it" tagged someone who had to chase him around the circle. If "it" was caught before he got back to the empty space in the circle, he had to go into the centre of the circle, which was called the mush pot, and the person who caught him became "it".

Ramona tried to stand next to the girl with the springy curls, but instead she found herself beside Howie. "I thought you were going to get a present," gloated Howie.

Ramona merely scowled and made a face at Howie, who was "it", but quickly landed in the mush pot because his new jeans were so stiff they slowed him down. "Look at Howie in the mush pot!" crowed Ramona.

Howie looked as if he were about to cry, which Ramona thought was silly of him. Only a baby would cry in the mush pot. Me, me, somebody tag me, thought Ramona, jumping up and down. She longed for a turn to run around the circle. Susan was jumping up and down too, and her curls bobbed enticingly.

At last Ramona felt a tap on her shoulder. Her turn had come to run around the circle! She ran as fast as she could to catch up with the sneakers pounding on the asphalt ahead of her. The *boing-boing* curls were on the other side of the circle. Ramona was coming closer to them. She put out her hand. She took hold of a curl, a thick springy curl—

"*Yow!*" screamed the owner of the curls.

Startled, Ramona let go. She was so surprised by the scream that she forgot to watch Susan's curl spring back.

Susan clutched her curls with one hand and pointed at Ramona with the other. "That girl pulled my hair! That girl pulled my hair! Ow-ow-ow." Ramona felt that Susan did not have to be so touchy. She had not meant to hurt her. She only wanted to touch that beautiful, springy hair that was so different from her own straight brown hair.

"Ow-ow-ow!" shrieked Susan, the centre of everyone's attention.

"Baby," said Ramona.

"Ramona," said Miss Binney, "in our

kindergarten we do not pull hair."

"Susan doesn't have to be such a baby," said Ramona.

"You may go sit on the bench outside the door while the rest of us play our game," Miss Binney told Ramona.

Ramona did not want to sit on any bench. She wanted to play Grey Duck with the rest of the class. "No," said Ramona, preparing to make a great big noisy fuss. "I won't."

Susan stopped shrieking. A terrible silence fell over the playground. Everyone stared at Ramona in such a way that she almost felt as if she were beginning to shrink. Nothing like this had ever happened to her before.

"Ramona," said Miss Binney quietly. "Go sit on the bench."

Without another word Ramona walked across the playground and sat down on the bench by the door of the kindergarten. The game of Grey Duck continued without her, but the class had not forgotten her. Howie grinned in her direction. Susan continued to look injured. Some laughed and pointed at

Ramona. Others, particularly Davy, looked worried, as if they had not known such a terrible punishment could be given in kindergarten.

Ramona swung her feet and pretended to be watching some workmen who were building a new market across the street. In spite of the misunderstanding about the present, she wanted so much to be loved by her pretty new teacher. Tears came into Ramona's eyes, but she would not cry. Nobody was going to call Ramona Quimby a crybaby. Never.

Next door to the kindergarten two little girls, about two and four years old, peered solemnly through the fence at Ramona. "See that girl," said the older girl to her little sister. "She's sitting there because she's been bad." The two-year-old looked awed to be in the presence of such wickedness. Ramona stared at the ground, she felt so ashamed.

When the game ended, the class filed past Ramona into the kindergarten. "You may come in now, Ramona," said Miss Binney pleasantly.

Ramona slid off the bench and followed the others. Even though she was not loved, she was forgiven, and that helped. She hoped that learning to read and write came next.

Inside Miss Binney announced that the time had come to rest. This news was another disappointment to Ramona, who felt that anyone who went to kindergarten was too old to rest. Miss Binney gave each child a mat on which there was a picture that matched the picture on his cupboard door and told him where to spread his mat on the floor. When all twenty-nine children were lying down they did not rest. They popped up to see what others were doing. They wiggled. They whispered. They coughed. They asked, "How much longer do we have to rest?"

"Shh," said Miss Binney in a soft, quiet, sleepy voice. "The person who rests most quietly will get to be the wake-up fairy."

"What's the wake-up fairy?" demanded Howie, bobbing up.

"Shh," whispered Miss Binney. "The wake-up fairy tiptoes around and wakes up the class with a magic wand. Whoever is the fairy wakes up the quietest resters first."

Ramona made up her mind that she would get to be the wake-up fairy, and then Miss Binney would know she was not so bad after all. She lay flat on her back with her hands tight to her sides. The mat was thin and the floor was hard, but Ramona did not wiggle. She was sure she must be the best rester in the class, because she could hear others squirming around on their mats. Just to show Miss Binney she really and truly was resting she gave one little snore, not a loud snore but a delicate snore, to prove what a good rester she was.

A scatter of giggles rose from the class, followed by several snores, less delicate than Ramona's. They led to more and more, less and less delicate snores until everyone was snoring except the few who did not know how to snore. They were giggling.

Miss Binney clapped her hands and spoke in a voice that was no longer soft, quiet and sleepy. "All right, boys and girls!" she said.

"This is enough! We do not snore or giggle during rest time."

"Ramona started it," said Howie.

Ramona sat up and scowled at Howie. "Tattletale," she said in a voice of scorn. Across Howie she saw that Susan was lying quietly with her beautiful curls spread out on her mat and eyes screwed tight shut.

"Well, you did," said Howie.

"Children!" Miss Binney's voice was sharp. "We must rest so that we will not be tired when our mothers come to take us home."

"Is your mother coming to take you home?" Howie asked Miss Binney. Ramona had been wondering the same thing.

"That's enough, Howie!" Miss Binney spoke the way mothers sometimes speak just before dinnertime. In a moment she was back to her soft, sleepy voice. "I like the way Susan is resting so quietly," she said. "Susan, you may be the wake-up fairy and tap the boys and girls with this wand to wake them up."

The magic wand turned out to be nothing but an everyday yardstick. Ramona lay quietly, but her efforts were of no use. Susan with her curls bouncing about her shoulders tapped Ramona last. It's not fair, Ramona thought. She was not the worst rester in the class. Howie was much worse.

The rest of the morning went quickly. The class was allowed to explore the paints and the toys, and those who wanted to were allowed to draw with their new crayons. They did not, however, learn to read and write, but Ramona cheered up when Miss Binney explained that anyone who had anything to share with the class could bring it to school the next day for Show and Tell. Ramona was glad when the bell finally rang and she saw her mother waiting for her outside the fence. Mrs Kemp and Willa Jean were waiting for Howie too, and the five started home together.

Right away, Howie said, "Ramona got benched, and she's the worst rester in the class."

After all that had happened that morning, Ramona found this too much. "Why don't you shut up?" she yelled at Howie just before she hit him.

Mrs Quimby seized Ramona by the hand and dragged her away from Howie. "Now, Ramona," she said, and her voice was firm, "this is no way to behave on your first day of school."

"Poor little girl," said Mrs Kemp. "She's worn out."

Nothing infuriated Ramona more than having a grown-up say, as if she could not hear, that she was worn out. "I'm *not* worn out!" she shrieked.

"She got plenty of rest while she was benched," said Howie.

"Now, Howie, you stay out of this," said Mrs Kemp. Then to change the subject, she asked her son, "How do you like kindergarten?"

"Oh – I guess it's all right," said Howie without enthusiasm. "They don't have any dirt to dig in or tricycles to ride."

"And what about you, Ramona?" asked Mrs Quimby. "Did you like kindergarten?"

Ramona considered. Kindergarten had not

turned out as she had expected. Still, even though she had not been given a present and Miss Binney did not love her, she had liked being with boys and girls her own age. She liked singing the song about the dawnzer and having her own little cupboard. "I didn't like it as much as I thought I would," she answered honestly, "but maybe it will get better when we have Show and Tell."

Story Time

Humphrey Carpenter

Each term, a different class at St Barty's took it in turns to look after the school library. Last term it had been Class Four, and they had left everything very tidy. All the books were in the right place, and the cards which showed who had borrowed what had been neatly filled in. They had made the library look bright and cheerful by putting up posters of famous authors.

This term it was Class Three's turn. Mr Majeika organized a rota, so that groups of four people at a time were on library duty for a week. Being on library duty meant you had to check that all the books were returned on time by the people who had borrowed them.

You also had to keep everything neat and orderly.

Thomas, Pete and Jody were put on library duty with Hamish Bigmore. "That's not fair, Mr Majeika," said Thomas. "You know what Hamish is like. He'll muck everything up."

Mr Majeika sighed. "He's got to be in somebody's group," he said, "and you three are tough enough to stand up to him."

Pete and Thomas were rather flattered by this, but Jody said, "It's no use being tough. What we need with Hamish is eyes in the back of our heads. The moment we turn our backs, he'll be up to something."

As it happened, the week in which Thomas, Pete, Jody and Hamish were on library duty was going to be rather a special one. St Barty's was holding a Book Week, and on the last day a children's author was coming to St Barty's to talk to the school. Her name was Penelope Primrose, and she was well-known for her picture books for very young children. They were about a rabbit called Little Bluebell.

"Yuck," said Pete, when he heard that she was coming to St Barty's. "Why do we have to have *her*?"

"Never mind," said Mr Majeika. "I'm sure it will be very interesting to hear how books are made. Now, mind you keep the library nice and tidy all week, but especially on Friday, when Penelope Primrose is visiting."

All week long, Thomas, Pete and Jody put away books, filled out borrowers' cards, straightened chairs and tables, and made sure there were displays of books for everyone to see. Much to their surprise, Hamish Bigmore actually helped them, with a friendly smile on his face.

At first, Thomas was suspicious. "Hamish must be up to something," he said. "It's not like him to do a job like this without complaining."

"I agree," said Pete. "There's definitely some trickery up Hamish's sleeve."

But Jody said, "I wish people would give Hamish a chance. People always expect him to behave badly, so of course he does. If someone encouraged him for a change, he might become a reformed character. Well done, Hamish!" she called out to Hamish, who had got some polish and a duster from one of the cleaning ladies, and was polishing a table.

"Thank you, Jody," said Hamish. "I'm glad there's someone who doesn't always think the worst of me."

"There you are," whispered Jody to Thomas and Pete. "What did I tell you? You've been hurting his feelings with all your remarks. Can't you see that, for once, he's really trying his best?"

Shamefaced, Thomas and Pete got on with their work.

On Friday morning, the day of Penelope Primrose's visit, the library was looking spick and span. There were vases of flowers on the tables, and a big poster of Penelope Primrose had been put up. All her books were on display on a table. She was going to come and talk to Class Three at the end of the morning. Her talks to the other classes would be given in their own classrooms, but she had said she wanted to see the school library, and as Class Three were on library duty, it was decided that she should meet them in the library itself.

At the beginning of the mid-morning break, Jody popped into the library to make sure everything was ready. It all looked very nice. When the bell rang, she went to Class Three's classroom for the lesson before Penelope Primrose's talk.

"Where's Hamish Bigmore?" asked Mr Majeika when the lesson began.

"He said he was feeling sick, Mr Majeika," said Pandora. "He's gone to lie down in the medical room."

It crossed Jody's mind that, as the medical room was next door to the library, it would be really easy for Hamish Bigmore to get up to mischief and spoil all their preparations for Penelope Primrose's visit. But she felt that, after all she had been saying to Thomas and Pete about how they should trust Hamish, she shouldn't be expecting the worst of him like this.

When the bell rang for the end of the lesson, Mr Majeika said, "Now, will you all please go to the library, and I'll go and fetch Penelope Primrose and take her there to meet you." So off they all trooped.

Mr Majeika went to the staffroom, where Penelope Primrose was drinking a glass of orange juice and talking to Mr Potter. "How do you do?" she said to Mr Majeika. "I told Mr Potter that I *never* drink strong grown-up drinks like coffee or tea. I'm just a little girlie at heart, and I like a little glass of milkie and a choccie bickie, or a little squeezie of orange juice. Oh, I have had *such* a sweet time this morning with all the little tiny tots. They *do* love my bookies! And have you got more little babes for me to meet, Mr Majeika?"

"Er, yes," said Mr Majeika, wondering what Class Three would make of Penelope Primrose. "Come this way, please." And he led her to the school library.

There seemed to be some sort of

disturbance going on. Mr Majeika could hear Jody shouting at Hamish. But when he opened the door and took Penelope Primrose in, there was a sudden hush. "Here we are, everyone," he said. "Here's Penelope Primrose to talk to you." He led her to a chair beside the table which was piled with her books.

"Hello, kiddie-widdies," said Penelope Primrose, sitting down. There was no reply. Class Three were stuffing handkerchiefs into their mouths and trying not to laugh. Mr Majeika looked round the library, puzzled. Then he saw that Penelope Primrose was sitting just beneath a poster of herself, on which someone had drawn a big beard and moustache.

"Hamish Bigmore—" began Mr Majeika. But Penelope Primrose, not noticing that anything was wrong, had begun her talk.

"Now, my little dearies," she was saying, "I'm going to tell you all how my little bookie-wookies are made – these little bookie-wookies here." And she pointed at the display

of her books on the table beside her.

At this, a roar of laughter broke out from Class Three. Mr Majeika looked at the books. Somebody had been altering the covers. The titles were supposed to be: *We All Love Little Bluebell, Little Bluebell Goes Shopping, Little Bluebell Meets the Fireman,* and *Little Bluebell in the Post Office.* Someone had used felt pens to change them to: *We All Hate Little Bluebell, Little Bluebell Goes Stark-raving Mad, Little Bluebell Meets Frankenstein,* and *Little Bluebell Gets Locked in the Loo.*

Penelope Primrose had seen the books, and was looking quite white in the face. "Such *wicked* little tots!" she gasped. "I feel quite faint. I must have a sniff of these flowers to make myself better." She thrust her nose into the bunch of flowers in the vase in front of her – and then gave a shriek, because tucked in with the flowers were several large stinging-nettles.

"Hamish Bigmore!" roared Mr Majeika. "I know this is your doing!" Everyone looked round to see what Hamish would say. But he was nowhere to be seen. As Mr Majeika had shouted his name, there had been a flash of light, and Hamish had vanished.

"I didn't mean to make him disappear," said Mr Majeika, half an hour later, after Penelope Primrose had been soothed and sent away in a taxi (she said she would never go to another School Book Week again).

"You *never* mean to make him disppear, Mr Majeika," said Pete. "But it keeps happening."

This was true. During his first term at
St Barty's, Mr Majeika had accidentally
turned Hamish Bigmore into a frog. Another
time, losing his temper with Hamish, he had
sent him magically into a television set.

"I'll run and check the fish tank," said Jody,
"just in case he's become a frog again. And
Thomas, you turn on the TV and try that, just
in case." But there were no frogs in the fish
tank, and no sign of Hamish in the television
programmes.

"He'll turn up," said Pete. "He always does,
more's the pity. Let's get these books tidied
away, Mr Majeika, and I'm sure he'll be back
before the end of afternoon school."

"All right," said Mr Majeika, though he
looked worried.

"I'll try and wipe the felt pen off the covers
of Penelope Primrose's books," said Thomas.
"I wonder if Hamish has drawn things inside
them too." He opened one of the books. "No,
it looks all right – no felt-pen scribbles. Hey,
wait a minute, what's this? I don't believe it.
Come and see."

Class Three and Mr Majeika gathered round, and Thomas held up the book. It was *We All Love Little Bluebell*, and he had opened it at a page which had a picture of Little Bluebell talking to two other little rabbits. Except she wasn't just talking to two other little rabbits. She was talking to two other little rabbits and Hamish Bigmore.

"That's Hamish – I'd know him anywhere, even in a drawing by Penelope Primrose," said Thomas.

"Try the rest of the book," said Jody. "See if he's in any of the other pictures."

Thomas turned the pages. Sure enough, wherever there were pictures, Hamish was in them. He was dancing hand in hand through the woods with Bluebell and her rabbit friends, helping them to bake fairy-cakes, and putting up Christmas decorations in Little Bluebell's cottage. He looked absolutely furious at being there.

"Poor old Hamish," laughed Pete. "And what about the words? Let's see if he's got into them too."

He had. This is how *We All Love Little Bluebell* now began: "Once upon a time there was a pretty little rabbit called Bluebell. She lived in a pretty little house in a pretty little wood, and she had three nice little friends called Little Snowdrop, Little Buttercup and Little Hamish."

"I bet he's loving every minute of it," giggled Thomas. "Do you think he's in the other Little Bluebell books too?"

He was. As they turned the pages, there was Little Hamish going shopping with Little Bluebell and the others, playing at fire-engines and postmen, and having a sweet little time.

"Do leave him there, Mr Majeika," said Pete. "You can send his mum and dad the Little Bluebell books, and then they'll know he's safe."

"Oh, do, Mr Majeika," said Thomas. "Just for a few days." But Mr Majeika shook his head.

"I'll have to fetch him out," he said. "If I can."

He shut his eyes and muttered some words. The Little Bluebell books began to shake and shiver, and from their pages out stepped Hamish Bigmore. And after him skipped Little Bluebell, Little Snowdrop and Little Buttercup.

"Wow," gasped Hamish. "You'll never guess where I've been."

Little Buttercup tugged at his hand. "Little Hamish! Little Hamish!" she piped. "Come back to Bluebell Wood, because it's time to have fairy-cakes for tea." She had a voice rather like Penelope Primrose.

"Naff off," said Hamish.

"Are we going to have Little Bluebell and her friends in Class Three?" asked Jody. "Wouldn't they be happier in the infants' class?"

"I'll try and get them back into the books," said Mr Majeika. "Wait a minute – what's going on?"

The other books on the library shelves were beginning to shake and shiver too, and other figures were starting to step from their pages. "Gosh," said Thomas, "isn't that Robin Hood?"

"And there's Toad, Mole, Rat and Badger," said Jody excitedly.

From some shelves at the back of the library, where science-fiction and fantasy were stored, came Superman, Batman, and the strange creatures from *Star Wars*, while a nasty smell suggested that Fungus the Bogeyman couldn't be far away.

"Oh dear," said Mr Majeika, "I seem to have made the spell to release Hamish too strong."

Soon the library was packed with peculiar beings, creatures from outer space, and characters from comic-books. There was the sound of breaking glass. "Watch it!" called Jody. "Hamish has teamed up with Dennis the Menace, and they've just smashed a window."

"It's fantastic, Mr Majeika," said Pete. "You ought to ring up the television people and the newspapers. Here's all these famous characters from the books, in real life."

"I know," said Mr Majeika doubtfully. "But I think there's going to be trouble pretty soon." Indeed, Captain Hook and several of the pirates from *Peter Pan* were already climbing out into the playground, intent on some mischief. Mr Toad was following them, chortling, "I spy motor cars outside! Poop poop! Just let me get my hands on them."

"Ladies and gentlemen and, er, creatures," called out Mr Majeika, "it's been delightful seeing you all, but would you, please, now go back into your books?"

There was a general muttering at this, and then a shout of, "No, we won't!"

"You can't blame them," said Thomas. "It must be very boring, being in the same book year after year, and going through the same adventures every time someone reads it."

"Well, I can't help that," said Mr Majeika anxiously. "They've got to get back on the pages at once, otherwise there may be awful trouble."

At that moment, Mr Potter opened the door of the library, peered inside at the strange collection of figures, and said, "Ah, Majeika, having a Parents' Morning, I see." He closed the door and went.

"It's lucky he didn't notice anything," said Pete. "If you can't persuade them to go back into the books, Mr Majeika, perhaps you can do it with a spell?"

"I'll try," said Mr Majeika, and shut his eyes.

"Poor things," said Thomas. "They haven't had much of a holiday. If they had any sense, they'd go back into different books."

Mr Majeika had begun to mutter to himself, and the room was growing dark and the books on the shelves were starting to shake again. But several of the book characters had heard Thomas. "What a good idea," called out Robin Hood. "Come on, Batman, why don't you and I do a swap?" And soon the library was loud with cries of "I'll have your book and you have mine," and "Get out of the way – it's my turn in this one," as two different characters fought to get into the same book.

At last it grew quiet, and the room became light again. Jody breathed a sigh of relief. "Well, that's all right then, Mr Majeika," she said.

Mr Majeika opened his eyes. "I hope so," he said.

"They've certainly all gone," said Pete. "But let's check everything's OK." He took one of the books off the shelf.

It was *Alice in Wonderland*, and he opened it at the page which ought to show Alice talking to the White Rabbit. But instead of the White Rabbit, the picture showed one of the creatures from *Star Wars*.

"There's something wrong with the words too," said Jody, looking over Pete's shoulder. "Alice's name has disappeared, and it's all about robots and things."

"And look at this," said Thomas, taking another book off the shelf. "It's *Black Beauty*, but a whole lot of characters from the *Beano* annual have got into the words and pictures."

"This is dreadful," said Mr Majeika. "They've really all been very naughty. How am I ever going to get them back into the right books?"

"I shouldn't bother," said Pete. "I'd got bored with most of the books in the library, but if they've all been changed, I'll start at the beginning and read right through them again."

"Me too," said Jody. "It'll make them much more exciting."

"Book Week is supposed to make books seem more interesting, isn't it?" said Thomas. "Well, Mr Majeika, you've certainly done that!"

George Starts School

Dick King-Smith

One morning, not long after George's fourth birthday, his mother was watching him as he sat at the breakfast table, reading the *Financial Times*. His father had just left for work, taking George's eleven-year-old sister Laura with him, to school.

"Just think, George," said his mother. "Only two more terms and then you'll be going to school too. You'll be a Rising-Five."

"I am aware of my age, Mother," said George, turning a page (with difficulty, for the newspaper was large), "and sometimes I feel it."

"You'll like school, won't you, George?" said his mother. George put down the

Financial Times with a sigh.

"The answer to that question," he said, "can only be hypothetical. Whether I shall 'like' school, as you put it, has yet to be proven. Judging by what I read of the new curriculum, I shall not."

"Why, is it too difficult?"

"Too easy," said George, and he picked up the newspaper once more.

It was his mother's turn to sigh, a sigh partly of resignation to the fact that George always had the last word, and partly of pride at her most unusual son. She sat drinking her coffee and remembering how fantastically early George had learnt to speak, how fluent he was in the English language when less than six months old. Neither she nor her husband had ever known (because Laura had never revealed it) that in fact George was holding long conversations with his sister a mere four weeks after his birth, when he knew a great deal more than she did, including his multiplication tables.

"It's a pity," she said reflectively, "that there's a seven-year gap between you and Laura. When you go to primary school, she'll have left."

"Just as well," said George.

"What do you mean? Don't you like your sister?"

"Mother," said George patiently. "I am in point of fact extremely fond of Laura, but I am perfectly accustomed to doing without her during the day. Things will be no different."

"Yes, but when Laura's at school, I'm always with you, George. I shan't be then. You'll be all alone."

"According to Laura," said George, "there are a hundred and fifty children at the school which I am to attend, not to mention all the teachers, the secretary, the dinner ladies, the caretaker and the odd-job man. I shall not be alone."

His mother remembered these last words on the day, eight months later, when she walked, holding George by the hand, through the playground full of hordes of rushing yelling children. She looked down at her little son, so much smaller, it seemed, than nearly all the others, and saw that he was frowning.

"It's sure to be strange at first, George," she said. "But I'll be here to fetch you after school. Don't worry."

"I am not worried, Mother," said George. "Merely appalled at the noise and general confusion. How childishly everyone is behaving."

*

In Class 5, the reception class, the teacher, who was also new at the school and had never before set eyes on George or any of the other children, was filling in her register. Everyone had been shown a peg to hang their coats on, and a locker to keep their things in, and given a place to sit, and some crayons and paper to draw on. As each new child in turn was called to the teacher's desk, she wrote down their names in the register and, if they knew them, their dates of birth.

"Now then, who are you?" she asked when it came to George's turn.

"My name," said George, "is George."

"And do you know when your birthday is, George?"

"It is April the first," said George.

"April Fool's Day," said the teacher smiling.

George did not smile.

"You will find," he said severely, "that I am nobody's fool."

Later, the teacher went round looking at the pictures the children had drawn. Some were of their animals, some of their houses, some of their parents, and one little girl had actually written MUM under her picture.

"That's very good!" said the teacher.

Then she came to George.

If people's eyes could really pop out of their heads, George's new teacher would have gone blind at that instant, for George's picture, minute in detail, was of a motorcycle. Under it was written in joined-up writing,

1988 Honda Goldwing Aspencade.

"George!" gasped the teacher. "What in the world . . . ?"

"I am interested in motorcycles," said George, "amongst other things. This is a Japanese tourer. It has a flat four 1182 c.c. engine, a 5-speed gearbox and transistorized ignition."

George's second day at school was spent in Class 4, and by the end of the week he was in Class I, among the ten- and eleven-year-olds. The children treated him with the awed respect they might have accorded to an alien from outer space, and the teachers were, quite simply, flabbergasted.

The headmaster had at first paid little heed to rumours of George's abilities, but that Friday was one that he never forgot.

In the morning, he taught Class I. At lunch time, he summoned George to his study.

"Sit down, George," he said in a kindly voice.

"I can't," said George.

"Why not?"

"I fear the chair is too high for me," said George, so the headmaster lifted him on to it.

"Now, George," he said. "I just want to ask you some questions. How old are you?"

"Four years and eleven months," said George.

"They tell me you can do joined-up writing."

"Up to a point," said George. "My physical skills are inferior to my mental abilities."

"Ah," said the headmaster in a shaky voice. "What about numbers?"

"Mathematics, d'you mean?" said George. "My knowledge is purely in the realm of

arithmetic so far. Algebra and geometry are treats in store for me."

"And reading?" croaked the headmaster.

"Reading," said George, "is something I find most enjoyable. There are a great many excellent children's authors published these days, but I must confess to a weakness for the older classics. Take for example *Alice in Wonderland*. What a work of fantasy!"

"Fantastic!" whispered the headmaster.

After lunch Class I was working on a project about South America, drawing maps and putting in the capital cities and principal rivers and mountain ranges. To be fair to the headmaster, he knew the names of the capitals of most of the countries of South America, but on one he momentarily stumbled.

"The capital of Guyana is . . ." he said. "Silly of me, it's slipped my mind. Look it up, someone."

"No need," said a very young but already familiar voice. "It's Georgetown."

That evening George went to bed early.

"I'm quite tired," he said to his parents and Laura. "It's been a busy week."

"It's amazing," said his father later. "To be in the top class, his first week of school!"

"He's top of the top class!" said his mother.

"He's miles cleverer than me!" said Laura proudly. "He won't need me for help with homework, I'll need him." George's mother sighed. This time it was a deep sigh of pure regret.

"I just wish he needed me still," she said.

146

"He never seems to now."

Just then there was an awful wailing from upstairs.

It was a terrified wailing, the cry of a very young child that desperately wants its mother.

"Mummy! Mummy! Mummy!" cried George from the darkness of his bedroom.

"I'm coming, my baby!" called George's mother. "Mummy's coming!" and she rushed upstairs to find George sitting up in bed, sobbing his heart out. This was not the confident self-assured know-it-all cleverest child in the school. This was just a frightened baby, and she cuddled him as fiercely as she had when he was only tiny and had never spoken a word.

"What is it, George darling?" she said as she mopped away his tears. "Did you have a bad dream?"

"I did, I did, Mummy!" sobbed George.

"What was it? Tell Mummy."

Gradually George's sobs turned to sniffles,

and then he blew his nose and said, "I dreamt we were doing a science test at school."

"A science test?"

"Yes, we do science in the new curriculum, you know. And there was a simple question in it that I couldn't answer, and I cried like a baby. I cried in the dream, and I was crying when I woke up. I really must apologize for behaving so childishly."

"Poor lamb!" said his mother. "What was the question?"

"It was the order of events in the cycle of the internal combustion engine," said George.

"Forget about it, George," said his mother sadly. "I expect there'll be lots of questions you won't know the answers to."

"Not if I can help it," said George.

"Anyway, don't worry. Just go back to sleep. Mummy's here."

"Oh, I shan't worry any more, Mother," said George in his usual confident tones. "I've remembered it now. It's Induction – Compression – Ignition – Exhaust," and exhausted, he lay back and went happily to sleep.

Ms Wiz Spells Trouble

Terence Blacker

Most teachers are strange and the teachers at St Barnabas School were no exception.

Yet it's almost certain that none of them – not Mr Gilbert, the headmaster, who liked to pick his nose during Assembly, not Mrs Hicks who talked to her teddies in class, not Miss Gomaz who smoked cigarettes in the lavatory – *none* of them was quite as odd as the new form teacher for Class Three.

Some of the children in Class Three thought she was a witch. Others said she was a hippy. A few of them thought she was just a bit mad. But they all agreed that there had never been anyone quite like her at

St Barnabas before.

This is her story. I wonder what *you* think she was . . .

As soon as their new teacher walked into the classroom on the first day of term, the children of Class Three sensed that there was something different about her. She was quite tall, with long black hair and bright green eyes. She wore tight jeans and a purple blouse. Her fingers were decorated with several large rings and black nail varnish. She looked as if she were on her way to a disco, not teaching at a school.

Most surprising of all, she wasn't frightened. Class Three was known in the school as the "problem class". It had a reputation for being difficult and noisy, for having what was called a "disruptive element". Miss Jones, their last teacher, had left the school in tears. But none of that seemed to worry this strange-looking new teacher.

"My name is Miss Wisdom," she said in a

quiet but firm voice. "So what do you say to me every morning when I walk in?"

"Good morning, Miss Wisdom," said Class Three unenthusiastically.

"Wrong," said the teacher with a flash of her green eyes. "You say, 'Hi, Ms Wiz!'"

Jack, who was one of Class Three's Disruptive Element, giggled at the back of the class.

"Yo," he said in a silly American accent. "Why, hi, Ms Wiz!"

Caroline, the class dreamer, was paying attention for a change.

"Why is it Ms . . . er, Ms?" she asked.

"Well," said Ms Wiz, "I'm not Mrs because I'm not married, thank goodness, and I'm not Miss because I think Miss sounds silly for a grown woman, don't you?"

"Not as silly as Ms," muttered Katrina, who liked to find fault wherever possible.

"And why Wiz?" asked a rather large boy sitting in the front row. It was Podge, who was probably the most annoying and certainly the greediest boy in the class.

"Wiz?" said Ms Wiz with a mysterious smile. "Just you wait and see."

Ms Wiz reached inside a big leather bag that she had placed beside her desk. She pulled out a china cat.

"That," she said, placing the cat carefully on her desk, "is my friend Hecate the Cat. She's watching you all the time. She sees everything and hears everything. She's my spy."

Ms Wiz turned to the blackboard.

"Weird," muttered Jack.

An odd, hissing sound came from the china cat. Its eyes lit up like torches.

"Hecate sees you even when my back is turned," said Ms Wiz, who now faced the class. "Will the person who said 'weird' spell it, please?"

Everyone stared at Jack, who blushed.

"I.T.," he stammered.

No one laughed.

"Er, W . . . I . . ."

"Wrong," said Ms Wiz. "W.E.I.R.D. If you don't know how to spell a word, Jack, don't use it." She patted the china cat.

"Good girl, Hecate," she said.

"How did she know my name?" whispered Jack.

The new teacher smiled. "Children, remember one thing. Ms Wiz knows everything."

"Now," she said briskly. "Pay attention, please. Talking of spelling, I'm going to give you a first lesson in casting spells."

"Oh, great," said Katrina grumpily. "Now we've got a witch for a teacher."

Hecate the Cat hissed angrily.

"No, Katrina, not a witch," said Ms Wiz sharply. "We don't call them witches these days. It gives people the wrong idea. We call them Paranormal Operatives. Now – any suggestions for our first spell?"

Podge put up his hand immediately.

"Could we turn our crayons into lollipops, please, Ms?" he asked.

"No," said Ms Wiz. "Spells are not for personal greed."

"How about turning Class Two into frogs?" asked Katrina.

"Nor are they for revenge. There will be no unpleasant spells around here while I'm your teacher," said Ms Wiz before adding, almost as an afterthought, "unless they're deserved, of course."

She looked out of the window. In the playground Mr Brown, the school caretaker, was sweeping up leaves.

"Please draw the playground," said Ms Wiz.

"Imagine it without any leaves. The best picture will create the spell."

Almost for the first time in living memory, Class Three worked in complete quiet. Katrina didn't complain that someone had nicked her pencil. Caroline managed to concentrate on her work. Podge forgot to look in his trouser pocket for one last sweet. Not a single paper pellet was shot across the room by Jack.

At the end of the lesson, Ms Wiz looked at the drawings carefully.

"Well, they're all quite good," she said eventually. "But I think I like Caroline's the best."

She took Caroline's drawing and carefully taped it to the window.

"Please close your eyes while I cast the spell," she said.

There was a curious humming noise as Class Three sat, eyes closed, in silence.

"Open," said Ms Wiz, after a few seconds. "Regard Caroline's work."

The children looked at Caroline's drawing.

It looked exactly as it had before, except that it was steaming slightly.

"Hey – look at the playground!" shouted Katrina.

Everyone looked out of the window. To their amazement, the leaves on the ground had disappeared. Mr Brown stood by his wheelbarrow, scratching his head.

"Weird," said Jack. "Very weird indeed."

"Yes, I'm afraid she is a bit odd," sighed the headmaster, Mr Gilbert, as he took tea one morning with Miss Gomaz and Mrs Hicks in the Staff Common Room.

"Those jeans," sniffed Miss Gomaz. "And I never thought I'd live to see *black* nail varnish at St Barnabas."

"But you have to admit she seems to have Class Three under control," said Mr Gilbert. "That's a whole week she has been here and not one child has been sent to my study. Not one window has been broken."

Mrs Hicks stirred her tea disapprovingly.

"It won't last," she said. "The Disruptive

Element will get the better of her. And there are some very strange noises coming from that classroom."

"I'd keep an eye on the situation if I were you, Headmaster," said Miss Gomaz.

Mr Gilbert sighed.

"Yes," he said wearily. "That's what I'll do. Keep an eye on the situation."

The fact is that Class Three, including the Disruptive Element, were having the time of their lives.

Every lesson with Ms Wiz was different.

"Now, Class Three," she would say, "I'm going to teach you something rather unusual. But remember – what happens in this classroom is our secret. The magic only works if nobody except us knows about it." Surprisingly, Class Three agreed.

So no one – not even parents or other children at the school – had any idea of the strange things that happened to Class Three.

They never heard how Caroline's picture of

the playground saved Mr Brown a morning's work.

They never heard how Jack's desk moved to the front of the class all by itself when Hecate spotted him talking at the back.

They never heard how Katrina flew around the class three times on a vacuum cleaner after she had complained that Ms Wiz couldn't be a real witch – sorry, Paranormal Operative – because she didn't ride a broomstick.

They never heard about the nature lesson when the class met Herbert, a pet rat that Ms Wiz kept up her sleeve.

But they did hear about the day when Podge became the hero of the class.

Nobody could keep *that* a secret.

Once every term, Class Three played a football match against a team from a school nearby, called Brackenhurst. It was a very important game and everyone from St Barnabas gathered in the playground to watch. Last term, Class Three had lost 10–0.

"That was because Miss Jones picked all the wimps," explained Jack.

"Because she was a wimp herself," said Caroline.

The rest of the class agreed noisily.

"*I'll* be manager," shouted Jack over the din.

Ms Wiz held up her hands like a wizard about to cast a spell.

"I'll be manager," she said firmly.

"But you don't know anything about football," said Jack.

"Ms Wiz knows everything," said Caroline.

"Creep!" muttered Katrina.

Hecate the Cat hissed angrily.

"All right, Hecate," said Katrina quickly. "I take it back."

"My team," said Ms Wiz, "is Jack, Simon, Katrina, Alex and—" She looked around the classroom and saw Podge's arm waving wildly.

"*No*, Ms Wiz," several of the class shouted at once. "Not Podge! He's useless!"

"– and Podge."

There was a groan from around the classroom.

"Here comes another hammering," said Jack gloomily.

For a while during the game that afternoon, it looked as though Jack's prediction had been right. After three minutes, Brackenhurst had already scored twice. Podge had been a disaster, falling over his own feet every time the ball came near him.

"Serves that Ms Cleverclogs right," said Mrs Hicks, who was watching the match with Miss Gomaz. "Look at her, jumping up and down like that, making herself look foolish in front of the kiddies. Anybody would think she was a child herself."

"It's embarrassing, that's what it is," agreed Miss Gomaz.

"*Do* something," said Caroline who was standing next to Ms Wiz.

"And what do you suggest, Caroline?" asked Ms Wiz whose normally pale face was now quite red.

"You know," whispered Caroline. "Something *special*."

"Oh, all right," sighed Ms Wiz. "I suppose a *little* magic wouldn't hurt."

At that moment, Podge blundered into one of Brackenhurst's players and knocked him over. Mr Gilbert, who was referee, blew hard on his whistle for a free kick against Class Three – but not a sound came out. In fact, the only sound to be heard was a faint humming noise from the direction of Ms Wiz.

"That's better," said Caroline.

Brackenhurst's players were still waiting for the whistle to blow when Podge set off with the ball at his feet. He took two paces and booted it wildly. It was heading several feet wide of the Brackenhurst goal when, to everyone's astonishment, the ball changed direction and, as if it had a life of its own, flew into the back of the net.

For a moment, there was a stunned silence. Then Ms Wiz could be heard cheering on her team once more.

"What a shot!" she shouted. "Nice one,

Podge! Go for it!"

"Appalling behaviour," muttered Mrs Hicks.

From then on, the game altered completely. Not even in his wildest dreams, when he had scored the winning goal for Spurs in the FA Cup Final, had Podge played so well. Soon even Jack was shouting, "Give it to Podge! Give the ball to Podge!" while the Brackenhurst players were screaming, "Stop the fat one! Trip him, someone!"

But nobody could stop Podge. Playing as if

he were under a spell, he scored three goals to give Class Three a great 3–2 victory.

After the game, the class gathered around Ms Wiz, shouting, cheering and singing songs.

"So much for her having her class under control," said Mrs Hicks. "They may win matches but Class Three are worse than ever with the new teacher."

Miss Gomaz had hurried over to Mr Gilbert.

"Just look at that, Headmaster," she said, pointing to Class Three, who were now singing "Ms Wiz is magic!" at the top of their voices. "It's nothing short of anarchy."

But Mr Gilbert wasn't listening. He was still studying his new whistle and wondering why it hadn't worked.

"This is all very difficult," said Mr Gilbert, puffing nervously on his pipe. He was sitting in his study with Ms Wiz, who at this moment was looking at him with an annoying little smile on her face. "Very awkward. You see,

Miss Wisdom – er, Ms Wiz – there have been, well, complaints."

"Goodness," said Ms Wiz brightly. "What on earth about?"

Mr Gilbert fumbled around with his pipe. Why *was* he feeling so nervous? Of course, he was always uneasy with women, but there were lots of women who were more frightening than Ms Wiz – Mrs Gilbert, for a start. The thought of his wife made the headmaster sit up in his armchair and try again.

"Firstly, there have been complaints about the way you look," he said, glancing at Ms Wiz. She was actually wearing black lipstick today.

"You find something wrong with the way I look?" asked Ms Wiz, who was beginning to be confused by this conversation.

"No, no," said Mr Gilbert, tapping his pipe on an ashtray. "I like . . . I mean, I don't . . . personally . . . Then," he said, quickly changing the subject, "there's what you teach. Your history lessons, for example."

"But Class Three loves history," said Ms Wiz. "We're doing the French Revolution at the moment."

"So I gather," said Mr Gilbert. "The entire class was walking around the playground yesterday shouting, 'Behead the aristocrats!' I'm told that Jack was carrying a potato on the end of a sharp stick."

Ms Wiz laughed. "They're very keen," she said.

"Perhaps you could move on to some other part of history – *nice* history," said the headmaster. "1066, the Armada, King Alfred and the cakes."

"Oh, no," said Ms Wiz. "We already have our next project."

"May I know what it is?" asked Mr Gilbert uneasily.

"Certainly," said Ms Wiz. "The Great Fire of London."

The headmaster gulped. Mrs Hicks and Miss Gomaz had been right. Ms Wiz spelt trouble.

"Perhaps," he said, "you could concentrate

on some other subject for the time being."

"Of course," said Ms Wiz. "We'll try a spot of maths for a while."

Mr Gilbert smiled for the first time that morning.

"Perfect," he said.

Maths, he thought to himself after Ms Wiz had left his study. That couldn't cause trouble. Could it?

"Now, Class Three," said Ms Wiz that afternoon. "I'm going to test you on your nine times table – multiplication and division."

There was a groan around the classroom. Nobody liked the nine times table.

"And to help me," continued Ms Wiz, "I've brought my friend Archimedes." She reached inside her desk and brought out a large white owl. "Archie's what they call a bit of a number-cruncher. He loves his tables," she said, putting the owl on top of the blackboard.

"Cats, rats and now owls," muttered Katrina. "This place gets more like a zoo every day."

"Archie is a barn owl," said Ms Wiz, ignoring Katrina. "An extremely mathematical barn owl. Place the waste-paper basket beneath him please, Caroline."

"Why, Ms Wiz?" asked Caroline.

"Wait and see," said Ms Wiz.

Caroline put the waste-paper basket beneath Archie who was now looking around the classroom, blinking wisely.

"Now, Podge," said Ms Wiz. "Tell Archie what five nines are."

"Forty-five," said Podge.

"Toowoo," went Archie.

"That means correct," said Ms Wiz. "Simon – nine nines."

"Eighty-one," said Simon.

"Toowoo."

"Now, Jack," said Ms Wiz. "Let's try division. A boy has 108 marbles. He divides them between his nine friends. What does that make?"

"It makes him a wally for giving away all his marbles," said Jack.

Archie looked confused.

"Try again, Jack," said Ms Wiz patiently.

"Erm . . . eleven."

Class Three looked at Archie expectantly. Without a sound, the owl lifted its tail and did something very nasty into the waste-paper basket beneath him.

"Uuuuuuuurrrrggghhhh, gross," said the children. "He's done a—"

"The correct word is guano," said Ms Wiz. "Jack?"

"Ten," said Jack.

Archie lifted his tail.

"Eight."

Archie did it again.

"How does he keep doing that?" asked Podge.

Ms Wiz shrugged. "He's well-trained," she said.

"We'd better have another basket standing by," said Katrina. "Jack's never going to get it."

"He'd better," said Ms Wiz firmly. "Every time Archie is obliged to do his . . . guano, it means fifty lines."

Jack groaned. "Um . . ."

Outside the door Mrs Hicks and Miss Gomaz were listening carefully.

They had left their classes with some reading work and were determined to catch the new teacher doing something wrong.

"Listen to that noise," said Miss Gomaz. "It's an absolute disgrace."

"Let's take a look through the window from the playground," said Mrs Hicks.

Moments later, the two teachers were watching in amazement as Jack struggled to give Archie the correct answer.

"There's a bird on the blackboard," whispered Miss Gomaz.

"It's . . . it's going to the lavatory," gasped Mrs Hicks. "In a bin. I can't believe my eyes."

They were just pressing their noses to the window-pane to get a closer look when Ms Wiz glanced up. Those at the front of the class could hear a slight hum coming from her direction.

"Miss Gomaz! Miss Gomaz!" said Mrs Hicks. "My nose! It's stuck to the glass!"

"Mine too!" cried Miss Gomaz, trying to pull back from the window-pane. "Ouch! That hurts!"

It was at that moment that the bell rang for afternoon break. Soon the teachers were surrounded by laughing children.

"Don't just stand there, you horrible children," screamed Mrs Hicks. "Get help quickly."

"No need," said Ms Wiz, who had joined the children in the playground. She tapped the glass. Miss Gomaz and Mrs Hicks fell back, free at last.

"It must have been the frost," said Ms Wiz, with an odd little smile.

"Frost?" said Miss Gomaz, rubbing her nose. "At this time of year? Don't talk daft."

"It's only September," said Mrs Hicks.

"Yes," said Ms Wiz. "What funny old weather we've been having, don't you think?"

Pippi Starts School

Astrid Lindgren

Pippi lives with her monkey, Mr Nelson, and a horse in a cottage called Villekulla. Her good friends Tommy and Annika live next door. As Pippi has no mother or father, she does whatever she likes, never having to bother about what adults say.

Quite naturally, Tommy and Annika went to school. Each morning at eight o'clock they trudged away hand in hand with their school-books under their arms.

At that hour Pippi was usually to be found riding her horse or dressing Mr Nelson in his little costume. Or she would be doing her morning exercises, which consisted of standing bolt upright on the floor and then turning forty-three somersaults in the air, one right after the other. After this she would sit on the kitchen table and enjoy a big cup of coffee and a cheese sandwich in peace and quiet.

Tommy and Annika always looked wistfully towards Villekulla Cottage when they toiled away to school. They would much, much rather have gone to play with Pippi. If only Pippi had had to go to school too, it wouldn't have been quite so bad.

"Just think what fun we could have together on our way home from school," said Tommy.

"Yes, and on the way there too," Annika agreed.

The more they thought about it, the more it seemed a pity that Pippi didn't go to school. Finally they decided to try and persuade her to begin.

"You can't *imagine* what a nice teacher we have," said Tommy artfully to Pippi one afternoon when he and Annika were visiting

Villekulla Cottage after having first done all their homework.

"Oh, if you *knew* what fun it is at school," said Annika innocently. "I should go out of my mind if I couldn't go!"

Pippi sat on a stool washing her feet in a tub. She didn't say anything, but just wiggled her toes a little so the water splashed around.

"One doesn't have to be there so *terribly* long," continued Tommy. "Just till two o'clock."

"Yes, and we get Christmas holidays and Easter holidays and summer holidays," said Annika.

Pippi bit her big toe thoughtfully, but didn't say anything. Suddenly, without hesitation, she tossed all the water out on the floor, so that Mr Nelson, who was sitting near by playing with a mirror, got his trousers absolutely soaked.

"It's unjust!" said Pippi sternly, without taking any notice of Mr Nelson's distress over the wet trousers. "It's absolutely unjust. I'm not going to stand for it!"

"Not stand for what?" asked Tommy.

"In four months it's Christmas, and you'll be getting Christmas holidays. But me, what do *I* get?" Pippi's voice sounded gloomy. "No Christmas holidays; not even the very teeniest Christmas holiday," she complained. "There's got to be a change here. Tomorrow I'm beginning school!"

Tommy and Annika clapped their hands with joy.

"Hurrah! Then we'll wait for you outside our gate at eight o'clock."

"No, no," said Pippi. "I can't begin *that* early. And for that matter, I think I'll be riding to school."

And she did. At exactly ten o'clock the next morning she lifted her horse down from the front porch, and a moment later all the people of the little town rushed to their windows to see what horse had run away. That is to say, they *thought* it had run away. But it hadn't. It was simply that Pippi was in a hurry to get to school. In a wild gallop she burst into the school yard, hopped off the horse at full speed, tied him with a string, and flung open the door of the school-room with a terrific crash that made Tommy and Annika and their classmates jump in their seats.

"Hey, hurrah!" shouted Pippi and waved her big hat. "Am I in time for pluttification?"

Tommy and Annika had explained to their teacher that a new girl called Pippi Longstocking would be coming. The teacher had also heard about Pippi from people in the town. As she was a very kind and pleasant teacher, she had decided to do everything she could to make Pippi feel at home in school.

Pippi flung herself down into an empty seat without anyone having asked her to do so. But the teacher took no notice of her careless manner. She just said in a friendly way, "Welcome to school, little Pippi. I hope you will be happy here and that you will learn a great deal."

"To be sure! And *I* hope I'll get Christmas holidays," said Pippi. "'Cause that's the reason I've come. Justice above all things!"

"If you'll first tell me your full name," said the teacher, "I shall enrol you in the school."

"My names is Pippilotta Provisionia Gaberdina Dandeliona Ephraimsdaughter Longstocking, daughter of Captain Ephraim Longstocking, formerly the terror of the seas, now Cannibal King. Pippi is really just my nickname, 'cause my father thought Pippilotta was too long to say."

"I see," said the teacher. "Well, then, we shall call you Pippi too. But now perhaps we should test your knowledge a bit," she continued. "You're quite a big girl, so you probably know a great deal already. Let us begin with arithmetic. Now, Pippi, can you tell me how much seven and five make?"

Pippi looked rather surprised and cross. Then she said, "Well, if *you* don't know, don't think I'm going to work it out for you!"

All the children stared in horror at Pippi. The teacher explained to her that she wasn't to answer in that way at school. She wasn't to call the teacher just "you" either; she was to call the teacher "ma'am".

"I'm awfully sorry," said Pippi apologetically. "I didn't know that. I won't do it again."

"No, I should hope not," said the teacher. "And now I'll tell you that seven and five make twelve."

"You see!" said Pippi. "You knew it all the time, so why did you ask, then? Oh, what a blockhead I am! Now I called you just 'you' again. 'Scuse me," she said, giving her ear a powerful pinch.

The teacher decided to pretend that nothing was the matter.

"Now, Pippi, how much do you think eight and four make?"

"I s'pose round about sixty-seven?" said Pippi.

"Not at all," said the teacher. "Eight and four make twelve."

"Now, now, my good woman, that's going too far," said Pippi. "You said yourself just now that it was seven and five that made twelve. There oughter be *some* order, even in a school! If you're so keen on this silly stuff, why don't you sit by yourself in a corner and count, and let us be in peace so we can play tag? Oh, dear! Now I said just 'you' again," she said with horror. "Can you forgive me this last time too? I'll try to remember better from now on."

The teacher said she would do so. But she thought that trying to teach Pippi any more arithmetic wasn't a good idea. She began to ask the other children instead.

"Can Tommy answer this question, please?" she said. "If Lisa has seven apples and Axel has nine apples, how many apples have they together?"

"Yes, answer that one, Tommy," Pippi chimed in. "And at the same time answer me this one: if Lisa has a tummy ache and Axel has even *more* of a tummy ache, whose fault is it, and where had they pinched the apples?"

The teacher tried to look as if she hadn't heard, and turned to Annika.

"Now, Annika, this problem is for you: Gustav went with his friends on a school outing. He had elevenpence when he went and sevenpence when he came home. How much had he spent?"

"All right," said Pippi, "then *I'd* like to know why he was so extravagant, and if it was a ginger beer he bought, and if he'd washed well behind his ears before he left home."

The teacher decided to give up arithmetic completely. She thought that perhaps Pippi would be more interested in learning to read. She therefore brought out a picture of a pretty little green island surrounded by blue water. Just over the island stood the letter "i".

"Now, Pippi, I'm going to show you something very interesting," she said quickly. "This is a picture of an iiiiiisland. And this letter above the iiiiiisland is called 'i'."

"Oh, I can hardly believe that," said Pippi. "It looks to me like a short line with a fly-speck over it. I'd like to know what islands and fly-specks have to do with each other."

The teacher brought out the next picture, which was of a snake. She explained to Pippi that the letter over it was called "s".

"Speaking of snakes," said Pippi. "I don't s'pose I'll ever forget the time I fought with a giant snake in India. It was such a horrid snake, you can't *imagine*; he was fourteen yards long and as angry as a bee, and every day he ate up five Indians and two little children for dessert. One day he came and wanted *me* for dessert, and he wound himself round me – krratch – but 'I've learned a thing or two at sea,' I said, and hit him on the head – boom – and then he *hissed* – uiuiuiuiuiuitch – and then I hit him again – boom and – ow— well – then he died. So *that's* the letter 's'?

Very interesting!"

Pippi had to catch her breath for a moment. The teacher, who was beginning to think Pippi a noisy and troublesome child, decided to let the class draw for a while. Surely Pippi would sit quietly and draw, thought the teacher. So she brought out paper and pencils and handed them out to the children.

"You may draw whatever you like," she said, and she sat down at her desk and began correcting copy-books. After a while she looked up to see how the children were getting on. They all sat looking at Pippi, who lay on the floor drawing to her heart's content.

"But, Pippi," said the teacher impatiently, "why don't you draw on the paper?"

"I used that up long ago. There isn't room enough for my whole horse on that silly little scrap of paper," said Pippi. "Just now I'm working on the front legs, but when I get to the tail I'll most likely be out in the corridor."

The teacher thought hard for a moment. "Perhaps we should sing a little song instead?" she suggested.

All the children stood up beside their seats; all but Pippi, who lay still on the floor.

"Go ahead and sing," she said. "I'm going to rest a bit. Too much study can break the healthiest."

But now the teacher's patience had come to an end. She told all the children to go out into the school yard, because she wanted especially to talk to Pippi.

When the teacher and Pippi were alone, Pippi got up and came forward to the desk.

"Do you know," she said, "I mean, do you know, *ma'am*, it was really lots of fun to come here and see what it's like. But I don't think I want to go to school any more, Christmas holidays or no Christmas holidays. There's just too many apples and islands and snakes and all that. I just get flustered in the head. I hope you're not disappointed, ma'am."

But the teacher said she *was* disappointed, most of all because Pippi wouldn't try to behave properly, and that no girl who behaved as badly as Pippi would be allowed to come to school even if she wanted to very much.

"Have I behaved badly?" asked Pippi, very surprised. "But I didn't know that myself," she said, looking sad. No one could look as tragic as Pippi when she was unhappy. She stood silently a minute, and then she said in a shaking voice, "You understand, ma'am, that when your mother is an angel and your father a Cannibal King, and you've travelled all your life on the seas, you don't really know *how* you oughter behave in a school with all the apples and the snakes."

Then the teacher said that she quite understood, and that she wasn't disappointed in Pippi any longer, and that perhaps Pippi could come back to school when she was a bit older. And Pippi said, beaming with pleasure, "I think you're awful nice, ma'am. And look what I've got for you, ma'am!"

Out of her pocket Pippi brought a fine little gold chain, which she laid on the desk. The teacher said she couldn't accept such a valuable gift from Pippi, but then Pippi said, "You have to! Else I'll come back again tomorrow, and *that* would be a pretty spectacle!"

Then Pippi rushed out into the school yard and leapt upon the horse. All the children crowded around to pat the horse and to watch her leave.

"I'm glad I know about Argentine schools," Pippi said in a superior manner looking down at the children. "You ought to go *there*! They begin Easter holidays three days after Christmas holidays, and when the Easter holidays are over, it's just three days till summer holidays. Summer holidays are over on the first of November. 'Course, then there's a bit of a grind until Christmas holidays begin on the eleventh of November. But it's not too bad, 'cause at least there aren't any lessons. It's strictly forbidden to have lessons in Argentina. It does happen once in a while that some Argentine child or other hides himself in a cupboard and sits there in secret and reads, but woe betide him if his mother finds him out! They don't have arithmetic in the schools there at all, and if there's a child who knows how much seven and five is, he has to stand in the corner all day if he's so stupid that he tells it to the teacher. They have reading on Fridays only, and then only in case they happen to have some books there. But they never do."

"Yes, but what do they do in school then?" asked a little boy.

"Eat sweets," said Pippi without hesitation. "A long pipe goes direct from a sweet factory in the neighbourhood to the school-room.

Sweets shoot out of it all day, so the children are kept busy just eating."

"But what does the teacher do?" asked a little girl.

"Picks the papers off the sweets, dunce," said Pippi. "Did you think they did it themselves? Hardly! They don't even as much as go to school themselves. They send their brothers."

Pippi waved her big hat.

"Yoicks, tally ho!" she cried. "You won't see me in a minute. But always remember how many apples Axel had, else you'll come to a bad end, hahaha!"

With ringing laughter Pippi rode out through the gate, so fast the gravel whirred around the horse's hooves and the school windows rattled.

Dragon in Top Class

June Counsel

Flying along the lane to school this sparkling September morning, Sam stopped at the Rec to look across at the baby swings because it was in one of those baby swings that he'd first seen Scales, the baby dragon, who was now his friend! A year ago today, thought Sam, and now I'm Top Class and Scales will be Top Class too.

He walked into the Rec and stood looking round. There were new baby swings, but not brightly coloured like the old ones. These had bars and seats of solid rubber, black or dull orange. Under the big swings, instead of concrete, were squares of the same solid rubber. The roundabout had gone and there was a new slide, much lower and tamer than the old one. There was now a seat for parents and a litter-bin. It was tidy and safe, but not exciting, and Sam was glad he'd known the Rec when the slide was high and there was a roundabout that could be whirled faster and faster and faster, because what one wants, thought Sam, is excitement.

He swished at the grass. Shining, winged things, seeds and insects, flew up and flickered away. He saw a feather quivering on a grass stem and picked it off; such a shining, shimmering morning as though the air were dancing.

"Oh, Scales," he called, "you would *love* it!" and – there *was* Scales with butterflies zigzagging between his spines and tiny beetles in jewelled wingcases running over his claws.

"I heard you call, Sam, and I thought, oh good, term's started. Hang on to my front claws and I'll hang-glide you to school."

He rose up, and Sam put up his hands and caught hold of the strong curved claws and –

wow – they were off! A glorious way to go to school, even though the air rushed past like iced water and he could hardly breathe.

Bump! Scales dropped him gently on to the Infant grass by the may tree and flew off.

The bell rang and Sam raced in and up the corridor to Class 1. Class 1 was like a barn, a big old classroom that had been the *whole* school when the school was first built. It had a high red wooden ceiling and brick walls. The two long walls were painted white. At one end was a raised wooden platform with a red-painted wall behind it and tall old windows. At the other end, the wall was painted green and had a green curtain right across its bottom half. Red and green, thought Sam excitedly. *Dragon* colours.

Coming in at the door, he twitched the curtain aside and gasped. Shelves and shelves and shelves piled with books, papers, boxes – all the things Mrs Green would want this term, and all the things that other teachers had wanted in other terms. It was green and dim and shadowy behind the curtain and Sam felt his spine tingle.

He dropped the curtain and walked up to the new Nature and Science Table and put his feather on it. Mrs Green nodded approvingly. "Because," she said, "this term we're doing Flight!"

"*Science*," corrected Christopher, who was clever. "We've got the National Curriculum at home and I've done some of the experiments already."

"Then we shall take flight on the wings of your knowledge," Mrs Green said airily. "Now, gather round everybody, and listen to your names and tables. Sam, you're on GLIDERS. That's the table over by the green curtain."

The curtain rippled gently, Mrs Green noticed. "This is a draughty old classroom. We shall have a job keeping warm."

Sam noticed, and felt warm with joy. *Scales* was there. He's blowing the curtain.

"Mrs Green, can Scales be in this term? He knows all about Flight."

"If he's good," said Mrs Green, who had

never seen Scales but knew that Sam loved him. "If he's helpful."

The curtain rippled again. "He will be," said Sam. "He's promised."

There was a commotion at the door. A mother pushed it open and dragged in a kicking, hitting, red-haired boy. Mrs Green hurried over to her. "Just go quickly," she said to the mother. "I'll take him."

She closed the door and said cheerfully, "Now, Russ, come and meet Ivy and Sebastian."

The red-haired boy flung himself flat on the floor. Mrs Green pulled him up and half-pushed, half-walked him to the ROCKETS table. "This is your chair, Russ." But the minute she let him go, Russ slid under the table. Ivy reached her hand under to haul him back and screeched, "Ow! He's bitten me."

A knock came at the door. Miss Barley the headteacher put her head round. "Mrs Green, a minute please."

Mrs Green said, "Class 1, help Russ while I go to Miss Barley." And went quickly out.

"You wicked boy!" stamped Ivy, sucking her hand. Russ put out a thumb and finger curved like a crab's claw and pinched her. Then he rushed for the door, but big Billy Bottom threw himself against it and stopped him. Sam started forward. "Russ, come and sit with us," but Russ jabbed him in the chest and began trying to tear Billy from the door. A claw came out from behind the green curtain and hooked Russ round the edge of it, quick as a wink.

There was complete silence. Ivy stopped

sucking, Billy stopped panting, everyone – so it seemed – stopped breathing.

Then, they heard a crunching, grinding noise and a huge swallow. Class 1 went white.

"Scales," shrieked Sam, "you mustn't eat him!"

Scales's voice said, "I'm just showing him what dragons *can* do." Then the curtain whipped up and Russ shot out. He walked jerkily to the ROCKETS table and sat down. No one spoke. Then Sebastian, who sat opposite him, said, "His eyes are very bright! He's – smiling!"

Mrs Green came back. "Oh, good children, what a lovely quiet classroom. Russ, your mummy's very worried, she wants to take you home—"

"NO," roared Russ, clenching his fist. "I WANT TO STAY HERE!"

"Well," said amazed Mrs Green, "we want you to stay! So that's good."

"It was Scales," Class 1 told her. "He helped."

"Oh, did he?" said Mrs Green. "Well, in that case . . . he can stay, but he'll find it very different from Class 4. In Top Class we're going to work very hard and learn a lot of different things, and he *won't* have his cave!"

"He doesn't need it. He's living behind the green curtain," Top Class said patiently, and pointed. The green curtain billowed gently.

"That's Scales blowing," Russ said.

"That's the draught under the door blowing," said Mrs Green. "Now, let us turn our minds away from Scales." A chuckle sounded behind the green curtain. Mrs Green looked round sharply, but the curtain (and Top Class) was still and straight. "You've all got a piece of paper in front of you. Fold it in four, now open it. You've got four squares. I want you to draw the four seasons, one in each square, because I want to find out whether you understand what we mean by seasons."

Top Class began to draw, but Russ put his red head down on the table and burst into tears. Mrs Green rushed over to him.

"I can't *do* all this learning," wailed Russ. "It's too much."

"Oh, but you can, we've got a whole *year* to do all this learning," Mrs Green put her arm round him. "We don't have to do it all at once. Little by little. You've no idea how clever we shall all be in a year's time!"

But when the pictures were finished, many were not all that clever. True, Billy Bottom had written *It is Spring, It is Summer, It is Autumn, It is Winter* at the bottom of his pictures, but his tree, in full leaf, stayed the same in all of them.

"It's no good drawing a caravan for summer, Ivy. People go off in their caravans in all seasons, even winter," Mrs Green pointed out. "And talking of winter, Weefy, why have you put a picnic in winter?"

"That's when we have them," answered Weefy, who came from an odd family. "There's too many flies in summer."

"Well, try again, Class. Have a *think*. Think what *trees* do, while I get on with my display."

She climbed up on to the platform and

began arranging books, pictures, photographs and objects under a notice that said: THINGS THAT TRAVEL BY AIR. Scales came tiptoeing out through the curtain and went up to the blackboard. He picked up the coloured chalks and began to draw soundlessly. The chalk didn't even squeak. It was like magic! Top Class watched, breathless with delight but, like the chalk, not even squeaking!

"Good children," praised Mrs Green, working away with her back to them. "What a quiet, hardworking class. Well done. Particularly you, Russ."

Scales finished his drawing, signed his name with a flourish, bowed to the children who raised their hands and clapped – soundlessly – and went smirking back behind the curtain.

Mrs Green turned round. "My goodness! Who did that?" She came quickly off the platform and walked up to the blackboard, for on the blackboard Scales had drawn in vivid colours and scratchy lines: Magic Mountain in Winter, snow-covered with the dragons asleep inside; Magic Mountain in Spring, the snow melting, flowers pushing through and the dragons coming out of their cave, yawning and stretching and smiling with pleasure; Magic Mountain in Summer, the sun blazing down and the dragons basking on the rocks with the forest below green and hazy in the heat; and Magic Mountain in Autumn with a great wind blowing and the dragons lighting bonfires of leaves with their fiery breath.

"Scales did it," shouted Top Class, laughing and clapping. Russ seized another bit of paper and began drawing furiously. "I'm going to copy it. I'm learning!"

"I see Scales *signed* it," said Mrs Green. "I shan't ask who *did* it," – at the green end of the room the curtain blew out vigorously – "but I will accept the nom-de-plume. That's French for pen name. Another word you might like to learn is pseudonym. That's when people write or draw under a name that isn't theirs." She wrote *nom-de-plume* and *pseudonym* on the board, but not on the picture.

"Can he stay?" asked Top Class earnestly. "Please, can Scales stay in Top Class?"

"Looking at that picture, yes," said Mrs Green. "It's clear, it teaches, it's funny, it's memorable. Scales can stay!"

Top Class cheered. The bell rang. Mrs Green laughed. And took her handbag off to the staffroom and Scales came out into Top Class Classroom, swelling and shining and smiling with conceit.

"Top Class Dragon! TCD, that's me!"

"Well, now," said Mrs Green, "gather round, Class, and tell me what's in this jar?"

She and Class 1 were sitting on the platform on the magic mat that Mrs Green had brought with her from Class 4.

"Nothing," cried everyone except Christopher, "it's empty."

But, "Air," said Christopher.

"Chris is right," smiled Mrs Green. "It looks empty, but it's not! It's full of air. Put up your hands, everybody. What can you feel?"

Class 1 put their hands up. Russ waved his so hard he hit Ivy on one side and skinny Dinny Delmont on the other. Slap! Ivy hit him back. Smack! Russ hit *her* back! The green curtain at the other end of the room bulged suddenly. Russ gasped, folded his arms, sat like a stone. The green curtain flattened and hung still.

"I can feel my hair move," cried tiny Tina. "I'm making a wind."

"Yes," said Mrs Green, "you can't *see* air, but it's there and you can use it to make things move."

She got off the platform and walked down the classroom towards the green curtain. Class 1 held its breath. When she got to it she put her hands up, twitched it apart and put her head in. (Oh, thought Sam, it's *two* curtains, not one.) At the door end of the curtain, Scales put his head out! Mrs Green went further in. Scales came further out. He winked at Class 1 and flew up to one of the rafters and stretched himself along it.

Class 1 waved to him.

"Stop fanning yourselves now, and come and sit at your tables," Mrs Green called, coming out of the curtains with her arms full of things.

Jennie the helper came in and went swiftly round the tables with Mrs Green, taking things out of boxes and putting them on the tables.

"Now then, we're going to do things with air! People with balloons on their tables, see if you can lift a book with your balloon. People blowing bubbles, see if you can blow a square bubble. People with straws and scissors and glue, make a windmill. Jennie will help you."

Sam, who loved making things, particularly things that worked and were useful, made a windmill and invented a way of cutting out all the sails at once. I'm getting cleverer, he thought, and was surprised, and pleased.

Sebastian blew soap bubbles through all the different bubble spoons – square ones, oval ones, triangular ones – but *all* the bubbles came out round. Russ put his reading book on top of his balloon and blew and blew till the balloon filled and – lifted the book up!

"Science is fun, and pretty, and clever," laughed Nargis, making a bubble picture like a field of summer flowers. "Scales would love it."

"Science is facts, Nargis," Mrs Green reminded her. "Scales is story and way above my head."

Above her head, Scales blew at the lights and Top Class laughed. The lights hanging from the rafters on their long chains swayed, and on the tables straws and paper rippled and lifted.

"Oh, this draughty classroom," cried Jennie, chasing paper.

"It isn't a draught," snapped Sebastian who was always tiresome and never more so than when he was cross and tired. "Look up there, it's—"

But Mrs Green looked down at her watch and cried, "Gracious, the bell will be going!

Clear away, everybody." So nobody looked up, but Scales looked down at Sebastian very hard.

When only Sam and Sebastian were left in the classroom, Scales flew down and picked up the triangular bubble spoon.

"Leave them alone," shouted Sebastian, who was tidying. "I'm putting them away."

But Scales put the spoon to his lips and blew two triangular bubbles. Then he swapped the triangular spoon for a round one ("Leave them *alone*," shrieked Sebastian) and blew a round bubble. The three bubbles floated together and made a—

"Bow tie!" cried Sam. "You're blowing a Sebastian, Scales!"

Sebastian clutched his bow tie and stared. Scales blew a big round bubble that settled on top of the bow tie bubbles, then he blew two bubble ears, two bubble eyes and a bubble mouth. Lastly he took the oval spoon (Sebastian too dumbfounded to say a word) and blew a long *oval* bubble and four long *thin* bubbles and there was a bubble boy, complete with body, arms and legs.

The bubble boy waved about, looking like a transparent Sebastian, only surprised instead of furious.

"Sebastian Bubblehead," said Scales. "Bubblehead and bubble*mouth*."

"Go away," shouted Sebastian furiously, "you can't *be* in this term. We're doing *Science*, we're doing *Air*."

"Air," said Scales, "is all you've *got* in your head." And he seized Sebastian under the

arms and took him for a hang-glide round the ceiling, diving in and out of the rafters and swerving between the lights, but Sebastian didn't enjoy it.

"Put him down, Scales, please," called Sam. "He'll be sick."

"I'm giving him air," cried Scales. "He was getting hot and red."

He glided down and dropped Sebastian in the bin. The bin fell over and Sebastian scrambled out, arms flailing. The bubble-Sebastian floated over to help, but Sebastian's flailing arms burst it and it spattered drops all over him.

"Now you've made me wet!" yelled Sebastian.

The door began to open. Scales shot up. Jennie walked in.

"Out you go, you two, or you'll miss play. I'll finish. Oh, what a mess."

Sam and Sebastian slipped out. Jennie set the bin up and put the rubbish back. She counted the bubble spoons. "One missing, the square one." She squatted down and looked under the tables. There was a tiny thud behind her. She swivelled round, saw the spoon lying near her and picked it up. Then she stood up – and gasped.

Hanging above the platform was a square bubble.

Jennie walked towards it, unbelieving. The bubble turned itself over and over to show its six sides. It was soapy, transparent, and square. Square, no doubt about it. It floated up and up – and burst!

"I don't *believe* it," Jennie cried.

And she didn't, though she'd seen it.

ACKNOWLEDGEMENTS

The editor and publishers wish to thank the following for permission to use copyright material:

Terence Blacker: for an excerpt from *Ms Wiz Spells Trouble*, first published by Piccadilly Press (1995) pp. 1–29, reproduced by permission of Macmillan Children's Books.

Humphrey Carpenter: for "Story Time" from *Mr Majeika and the School Book Week* by Humphrey Carpenter, first published by Viking (1992). Copyright © Humphrey Carpenter 1992, reproduced by permission of Penguin UK.

W.J. Corbett: for "Miss Parson's Pet" from *The Dragon's Egg and Other Stories* by W.J. Corbett, first published by Hodder Children's Books (1996), reproduced by permission of Hodder and Stoughton Ltd.

June Counsel: for "Wings" and "Bubbles", which occur as one story in this volume, from *Dragon in Top Class*, first published by Doubleday (1994). Copyright © 1994 June Counsel, reproduced by permission of Transworld Publishers.

Sita Heti: for "Cyclone", first published in *School Journal*, Part 4, No. 2 (1990). Copyright © 1990 Sita Heti, reproduced by permission of Learning Media Ltd, Wellington, and the author.

Dick King-Smith: for "George Starts School" from *Philibert the First and Other Stories* by Dick King-Smith, first published by Viking (1994), reproduced by permission of A.P. Watt Ltd on behalf of Fox Busters Ltd.

Astrid Lindgren: for "Pippi Starts School" from *Pippi Longstocking* by Astrid Lindgren, first published by Oxford University Press (1954), reproduced by permission of Oxford University Press.

Magdalen Nabb: for "Josie Smith's New Teacher" from *Josie Smith at School* by Magdalen Nabb, first published by Collins Children's Books (1990), reproduced by permission of HarperCollins Publishers Ltd.

Chris Powling: for "The Ghost Gorilla" included in *Snake on the Bus and Other Pet Stories*, first published by Methuen (1994). Copyright © Chris Powling 1994, reproduced by permission of David Higham Associates on behalf of the author.

Every effort has been made to trace the copyright holders but where this has not been possible or where any error has been made the publishers will be pleased to make the necessary arrangement at the first opportunity.

More amazing stories can be found in

Animal Stories
for Seven Year Olds

Chosen by Helen Paiba

Exciting stories include:

Delilah the spider's dreadful day

The boy who turned into a dog

Jeffy, the burglar's cat

The bears who came to dinner

Hedley the mouse's narrow escape

More fantastic stories can be found in

Funny Stories
for Seven Year Olds

Chosen by Helen Paiba

Hilarious stories include:

The crocodile and the runaway roller skates
The spider that had too many legs
The missing nose
The parrot that couldn't stop eating
The giant wiggly worm hunt

More amazing stories can be found in

Adventure Stories for Seven Year Olds

Chosen by Helen Paiba

Exciting stories include:

How Pirate Horrible became a hero

The legs that ran away

The Wolf Men's special dog

There's a monster in the dustbin!

The heart that wouldn't beat

More super stories can be found in

School Stories for Eight Year Olds

Chosen by Helen Paiba

Top-class stories include:

Teacher's froggy fright

The too-high gym jump

Danger in the playground

The crazy name confusion

More fantastic stories can be found in

Funny Stories
for Eight Year Olds

Chosen by Helen Paiba

Hilarious stories include:

The Unidentified Flying Dog

The man who couldn't stop laughing

The amazing talking baby

The boy who turned into a frog

The exploding Jelly Custard Surprise

Books in this series available from Macmillan

The prices shown below are correct at the time of going to press. However, Macmillan Publishers reserve the right to show new retail prices on covers which may differ from those previously advertised.

Funny Stories for Seven Year Olds	0 330 34945 7	£3.99
Animal Stories for Seven Year Olds	0 330 35494 9	£3.99
Scary Stories for Seven Year Olds	0 330 34943 0	£3.99
Adventure Stories for Seven Year Olds	0 330 39139 9	£3.99
School Stories for Seven Year Olds	0 330 48378 1	£3.99
Funny Stories for Eight Year Olds	0 330 34936 5	£3.99
Animal Stories for Eight Year Olds	0 330 35495 7	£3.99
Scary Stories for Eight Year Olds	0 330 34944 9	£3.99
Adventure Stories for Eight Year Olds	0 330 39140 2	£3.99
School Stories for Eight Year Olds	0 330 48379 X	£3.99

All Macmillan titles can be ordered at your local bookshop or are available by post from:

Book Service by Post
PO Box 29, Douglas, Isle of Man IM99 1BQ

Credit cards accepted. For details:
Telephone: 01624 675137
Fax: 01624 670923
E-mail: bookshop@enterprise.net

Free postage and packing in the UK.
Overseas customers: add £1 per book (paperback)
and £3 per book (hardback).